JEDI QUEST

THE CHANGING OF THE GUARD

JEDI QUEST

CHOSEN BY FATE.
DESTINED FOR CONFLICT.

#1 THE WAY OF THE APPRENTICE

#2 THE TRAIL OF THE JEDI

#3 THE DANGEROUS GAMES

#4 THE MASTER OF DISGUISE

#5 THE SCHOOL OF FEAR

#6 THE SHADOW TRAP

#7 THE MOMENT OF TRUTH

SPECIAL HARDCOVER EDITION: PATH TO TRUTH

STAR WARS

JEDI QUEST

BY JUDE WATSON

THE CHANGING OF THE GUARD

SCHOLASTIC INC.

New York   Toronto   London   Auckland   Sydney
Mexico City   New Delhi   Hong Kong   Buenos Aires

www.starwars.com
www.scholastic.com

No part of this work may be reproduced, stored in a retrieval system, or transmitted in any form or by any means, electronic, mechanical, photocopying, recording, or otherwise, without written permission of the publisher. For information regarding permission, write to Scholastic Inc., Attention: Permissions Department, 557 Broadway, New York, NY 10012.

ISBN 0-439-33924-3

Cover art by Alicia Buelow and David Mattingly.

SCHOLASTIC and associated logos are trademarks and/or registered trademarks of Scholastic Inc.

12 11 10 9 8 7 6 5 4 3 2 1   4 5 6 7 8 9/0

Printed in the U.S.A.
First printing, March 2004

STAR WARS®

JEDI QUEST

THE CHANGING OF THE GUARD

Senate aide Tyro Caladian winced at the look of frustration on the face of his friend Obi-Wan Kenobi. "I'm sorry," he said for the third time. "There is nothing I can do."

Obi-Wan wanted to groan. He wanted to kick a hole through the rare laroon wood paneling of Meeting Room A3000291 in the Senate. He wanted to react like a privileged, arrogant Senator used to getting his way. He wanted to lash out.

But he was a Jedi. Jedi did not do such things. They accepted even the most nerve-torturing frustrations with calm focus and unswerving direction. He must look for the flaw in the logic, discover the opening in the locked gate. Find the way. Petty emotions would only divert him. Obi-Wan took a deep breath and searched for his calm center.

He looked over at his apprentice, Anakin Skywalker. If Obi-Wan merely *felt* like kicking a wall, it appeared that Anakin would do so at any moment. His gaze was turbulent, boiling. Then, as Obi-Wan watched, a mask slid over Anakin's frustration. He looked composed now, perfectly in control.

An impressive achievement. Obi-Wan had noted Anakin's growth over the past six months while they had been tracking the evil scientist Jenna Zan Arbor from her last known stop in the Vanqor system. Anakin was seventeen now. He was becoming a man as well as a Jedi.

Together they had followed Zan Arbor's trail, tracing rumors and finding clues. They knew the scientist did not have access to her large fortune, which the Senate had confiscated and then dispersed among the many planets she had wronged. They knew what the Vanqors had paid her would soon be depleted. But they also knew that she had a taste for extravagance. She liked to live well. Perhaps she would leave a trail that way.

Obi-Wan and Anakin had found other missions along the way, places where they were needed that couldn't be ignored. Still they continued to search the galaxy for clues to Zan Arbor's whereabouts, occasionally diverted but never deflected from their goal.

The big break came when Anakin discovered she had bought a limited-production cruiser called a Luxe Flightwing. The ship was so rare and beautiful that everyone remembered it — fuelers on obscure space-ports, repair personnel in busy capital cities, customs officials, and especially other pilots. It had been an un-wise move, typical of her greed and arrogance. She wanted what she wanted, then she acquired it. But it was a bad mistake. Bit by bit, information trickled in, and at last they had tracked her to Romin, a small planet in the Mid-Rim.

Before traveling there to arrest her, Obi-Wan asked his friend and fellow Jedi, Siri Tachi, to help. Siri and her Padawan, Ferus Olin, had been involved in the search from time to time but had been called on by the Jedi Council for other missions. Still, Siri had pledged her support to Obi-Wan. Whenever he needed her for the final capture of Zan Arbor, she would be there.

Now in Meeting Room A3000291, Siri didn't show her frustration, but he sensed it in the taut lines of her muscled body. Obi-Wan knew all too well how Siri despised having to deal with the bureaucracy of the

Senate. She was always geared for action. In many ways, she was like Anakin.

"Look," she said to Tyro, "we're not stupid. We know it will be tricky. Romin is ruled by Roy Teda, who by all accounts is an evil dictator. It's not like he's going to invite the Jedi in. But the Senate is committed to arresting Zan Arbor. Why won't they give us permission to go in?"

"It's more complicated than that," Tyro said. Clearly uncomfortable under the scrutiny of Siri's blazing blue eyes, the Svivreni fiddled with the thick metal clasp that held his long black hair in a plume that ran down his back. Then he smoothed the glossy fur on his small, pointed face. "Senate procedure always is. Teda himself is in violation of several galactic laws. He imprisons without trial. We are certain he uses torture to extract information. He has shut down the information bureaus and controls the only communications system on the planet. He has even raided his planet's treasury for his own personal use."

"Exactly," Siri said impatiently. "He is a criminal. So why do we have to listen to him?"

"Because he is a duly elected ruler," Tyro said.

"But he rigged the elections!" Anakin burst out.

"That makes no difference," Tyro answered. "We must

still obey the laws of Romin. And there is a law forbidding any bounty hunters to enter."

"We are not bounty hunters," Ferus said. His dignity rang through his words. "We are Jedi."

Tyro swallowed. "Yes," he said, "but the law says that *no one* can arrest or transport a galactic criminal off Romin. And that's what you mean to do. Teda has made himself wealthy by offering his planet as a refuge to the most-wanted criminals. They're happy to pay him a hefty bribe in order to relocate to his planet. In return, he makes sure that any bounty hunters are forcibly expelled. If his security police find them, they are made to 'disappear.'"

"Then we'll just go to Romin without Senate approval," Anakin said.

Ferus frowned. Obi-Wan noted how Anakin bristled when he saw it. The two had never gotten along, and Obi-Wan wasn't surprised. Ferus followed the rules. Anakin had no hesitation about bending them to get a job done.

"Ah," Tyro said carefully, "I'm afraid that you *do* need approval. Without legitimate cause, you will be asked to leave the planet. And if you do not leave, it is likely you will be imprisoned — if you are lucky. Teda has been known to execute without trial."

"But the Senate cannot shield a criminal like Zan

Arbor!" Obi-Wan leaped to his feet and began to pace out his frustration. Now he knew why Zan Arbor had risked buying such a showpiece transport. She didn't care, because she knew she would be protected. That infuriated him. No one was above galactic law. "There has to be a way."

Tyro shook his head. "If there is, I can't think of it. The Senate looks the other way when it comes to Romin. The Romin Senator wields great influence. He is a favorite of Sano Sauro — who as you well know is the leader of a large voting bloc."

Obi-Wan groaned. "Not him again." He had tangled with Sano Sauro before.

"If you land on Romin secretly, you will be in violation of Senate laws," Tyro said. "And I assure you, the Senator from Romin will not hesitate to prosecute even a Jedi," Tyro spoke softly. "I'm afraid this is typical of the Senate these days. I am so sorry, my good friend Obi-Wan, that I cannot help you."

"I am grateful for what you've done," Obi-Wan said woodenly. He refused to accept that Zan Arbor was untouchable. As his Master, Qui-Gon Jinn, had said, *There is always another way.*

Tyro sighed. "I come from a peaceful world. The growing lawlessness in the galaxy troubles me greatly.

The prison worlds are not well maintained. Just recently there was yet another escape from a high-security prison, the Greylands Security Complex on Tentator. It was a notorious gang who broke free. Luckily the gang members were tracked and apprehended just hours ago. But such successes are rare, I must admit."

Obi-Wan stopped pacing and fixed Tyro with a keen gaze. "Who are they?"

"They are called the Slams," Tyro said.

"Species?"

"Humanoid. From Mamendin, in the Core. They started there with con jobs, ID thefts, things like that. Then they roamed the galaxy, mostly in the Core, pulling scams. They were the gang who heisted the entire treasury of Vuma. The leaders are fairly young — a man named Slam and a woman named Valadon. Slam is a con man and Valadon is an ID theft expert. They have only two other members — they keep their numbers small to maintain loyalty. The Slams were caught when they tried to break into a security vault of the Commerce Guild. You just don't go after the Commerce Guild without major consequences."

"I remember the Vuma affair," Siri said. "We heard about it at the Temple. It just about bankrupted the planet. The crystalline vertex they stole is still missing." She gave Obi-Wan a curious glance. "What is it? You've got that look on your face."

"What look?"

"That look that says, *You're going to hate this idea, Siri, but I'm going to do it anyway*," Siri said dryly.

Obi-Wan grinned. "Relax. You're going to love it."

CHAPTER TWO

Anakin looked over at his Master. They had grown even closer over the past months. Anakin had broken down after the mission on Vanqor and confessed his fears to Obi-Wan. He had been afraid to tell his Master how there were times he no longer wanted to be the Chosen One. He realized that he had been walking around with a nameless dread in his heart. He didn't know what he feared, but he knew that he lived with the fear every waking moment. Saying this out loud had shocked his Master, but it had freed Anakin in a way he still didn't understand.

Perhaps it had been his experiences in the prisoner-of-war camp on Vanqor that had caused him to unburden his heart to Obi-Wan. Whatever the reason had been, it had changed something between them. They had grown closer. They were truly Master and Padawan now.

He knew what had happened was a classic step in the Master–Padawan relationship. *The apprentice invites the Master, and it begins.* As learners, they had all wondered what the expression meant. The Master was the one to invite a Jedi student to be his or her apprentice. That was how it started. So what was the meaning of *The apprentice invites the Master?*

Now he understood. He had been Obi-Wan's apprentice for years before he had truly trusted him with the inner workings of his heart and mind. Once he had invited Obi-Wan to share his deepest fears, his worst nightmares, their relationship had shifted and deepened. It was as though they were starting again. *It begins.* Obi-Wan had told him that the same thing had happened with him and Qui-Gon. "In the middle of our journey together, we began again," he'd told Anakin.

It was mysterious and wonderful. They knew what each other would do before it was done. They knew what was in each other's thoughts. Whereas before Anakin would worry about what was on Obi-Wan's mind, now he accepted that some things he knew, and some things he didn't, and that many things on Obi-Wan's mind had nothing to do with him.

He could not read Obi-Wan's thoughts right now. He had no idea what his Master was planning. He felt just as puzzled as Siri. But where Siri felt worried, Anakin felt excited.

Siri raised an eyebrow. "I'm listening."

"We have a way to land on Romin and get to Jenna Zan Arbor, then get her off-planet without violating any Senate regulations or the laws of Romin," Obi-Wan said. "Technically."

"Technically?" Tyro asked.

"We enter legally," Obi-Wan said. "As criminals."

Siri sat down and slung one ankle over her knee. "Well, that's a relief. For a minute there, I thought you actually had a plan that made sense."

"We take on the identities of the Slam gang," Obi-Wan said. "I'll be Slam, you'll be Valadon. Anakin and Ferus can be the other two."

"Waldo and Ukiah," Tyro supplied. "But technically —"

"So, we land on Romin and find Zan Arbor," Siri said. "What next?"

"Well, I haven't planned it out completely," Obi-Wan said. "We find a way to lure her off-planet. That can't be too hard."

"Sure," Siri said. "One of the shrewdest scientific minds in the galaxy is going for a joyride with us. As Garen would say, piece of sweetcake."

"We'll think of something to tempt her to join us," Obi-Wan said. "The point is to land on Romin and contact her. We can only do that as criminals."

"Can I return to 'technically'?" Tyro asked. "Technically, you'd still be in violation of several laws I can easily think of. If you get caught."

"We're not going to be caught. That's where you come in," Obi-Wan said, turning to him.

Suddenly, Tyro looked uneasy. "Oh."

"We'll need ID docs and descriptions and background information," Obi-Wan said. "And you said they operated on different planets in the Core. That means they probably have a spaceworthy ship. Do you think you can pull some strings for us and commandeer it?"

"I don't know," Tyro said doubtfully. "That would take some favor trading."

"Your specialty," Obi-Wan pointed out.

"It would all have to be top secret, so I'd have to go to the Senate security committee first," Tyro said slowly. "They'd have to give me a waiver to approach the Overseer of Prison Worlds, who would have to issue an edict to the prison world's Confiscation Authority. . . ."

"I don't need the details, Tyro," Obi-Wan said. "I just need results. We'll also need time. You'll have to get the authorities to agree to keep the capture of the Slam gang a secret until we've completed the mission. They have to still be listed as escaped, in case anyone checks."

Tyro frowned. "That might be difficult. When they catch criminals, they like to boast about it. I'd need an indefinite Stop Comm order from the Central Posting Service —" Tyro caught Obi-Wan's eyes. He shut his datapad briskly and rose. "I'd better get started."

Tyro hurried out of the room.

"We'll have to clear this with Master Windu," Siri said. "And I'd bet it will take some persuasion."

"He'll agree," Obi-Wan said confidently. "He knows how important the capture of Zan Arbor is to the safety of the galaxy."

Anakin felt a surge of excitement as Obi-Wan and Siri began to discuss possible courses of action and how soon they could leave. The frustration of locating Zan Arbor but not being able to take her into custody was over. Now they had a focus. They had a way to apprehend her.

He pushed away the thought of seeing her again. Anakin had focused his attention on catching her. He had not thought about what he would do when they found her. He had met Jenna Zan Arbor in the prisoner-of-war camp on Vanqor. She had been pleasant, polite. Yet the memory of what happened there chilled him. She was the inventor of a drug that induced what she called the Zone of Self-Containment. Anakin had felt pleasure and contentment while under its influence. Nothing had bothered him. For the first time in his life, he had felt at peace. It was the feeling he had hoped to achieve as a Jedi. What had scared him was the thought that he would never feel that again. He had achieved true serenity in the Zone, but it had been a cheap victory, for after it was over, it had left him with guilt and fear. The very emotions he had tried to escape from.

Focus on the first step. The others will follow.

Much good had come out of his experience on Vanqor. The Zone had broken him down in a way that had been helpful. He had felt vulnerable and afraid, and he had leaned on his Master. He had come to see that Obi-Wan cared for him a great deal. His Master would be there for him always. That had been a great gift to carry away from an uncertain time.

Anakin tore his mind away from his own preoccupations and noticed that Ferus looked as though he were debating whether to speak. Anakin hoped he wouldn't. He rarely liked what Ferus Olin had to say.

Siri noted her Padawan's hesitation. "Is there something on your mind, Ferus?" she asked.

"I am just wondering if this plan is appropriate for the Jedi," Ferus said. "It is not for me to question Jedi Masters. . . ."

"Questioning is part of the role of an apprentice," Obi-Wan said kindly. "Go ahead."

"This isn't the kind of thing that a Jedi should do," Ferus said stiffly, obviously uncomfortable at second-guessing his Master. "Impersonating criminals? We are not tricksters. We are ambassadors of peace and justice."

Anakin wanted to roll his eyes. Ferus was such a show-off. He always had to bring up Jedi rules, as if he was the only one who remembered them. Did it ever occur to him that the important thing was to get the job done? Anakin looked over at Siri. She was nodding thoughtfully, as though she was truly considering Ferus's point. He wondered if she was just trying to be a good Master when she really wanted to call him a pompous bore.

"Of course that is true," Siri said. "But the galaxy is complex. The Jedi must operate differently and take different kinds of risks. There are planets that do not welcome our presence, yet circumstances demand that we help for the good of the galaxy." She sighed. "I have gone undercover before, Ferus. The Council decided that it was the only way to infiltrate a vast space pirating operation. I had to pretend to leave the Order. It was difficult. Every Jedi thought I had turned to the dark side, even Obi-Wan."

"It was a great act of bravery on Siri's part," Obi-Wan said.

"Every second of my deception went against my core," Siri continued. "I don't like lies. To live a lie takes a toll. Yet am I glad I did it? Yes. The Jedi were able to bring down a vicious pirate and liberate hundreds of slaves."

"I tangled with Jenna Zan Arbor before, when I was your age," Obi-Wan told Ferus. "She is a great enemy of the Jedi. She imprisoned Qui-Gon and drained his life in order to study the Force. She almost killed him. She *has* killed others. She is capable of anything. With the Zone of Self-Containment she could subdue an entire population. We must use any means to stop her."

"Any means?" Ferus asked.

There was a silence. Anakin saw Obi-Wan exchange a quick glance with Siri. Everyone in the room was thinking the same thing. *Means equal ends.* It was one of the core beliefs of the Jedi. In order to do good, one must act rightly at every step. If the means used were wrong, then the outcome was wrong, too.

"I did not choose my words carefully," Obi-Wan said. "My meaning is this — if we must use a little deception to catch her, then we will. In this case, our only hope is to beat Zan Arbor at her own game. She could consolidate her power on Romin. She could use the planet as a base for operations, thinking she cannot be touched there. She could do vast amounts of damage. Lives are at stake. Perhaps millions of lives." Obi-Wan's keen stare fixed on Ferus. "Don't you think that is worth forsaking your dignity and taking another's identity for a few days?"

Ferus's cheeks colored. Anakin realized that Obi-Wan had put a sure finger on the spot that was most tender in Ferus. His dignity. Obi-Wan had done it kindly, but Ferus had felt a sting.

Ferus nodded. "I will, of course, do as you say."

"But you must believe it, too," Siri said.

After a short pause, Ferus said, "I do. I trust that those with more wisdom know the way."

Ferus seemed to be sincere. He was incapable of lying. Yet it was clear that Siri and Obi-Wan had not done away with all of his uneasiness.

Obi-Wan turned back to Siri and Anakin. "If all goes well, we can brief Master Windu and leave tonight," he said.

Anakin nodded. He bent his head closer to Siri and Obi-Wan as they discussed their next step. Ferus was silent throughout their entire discussion. For once, Ferus was the outsider. For once, it wasn't him.

CHAPTER THREE

Tyro did not tell Obi-Wan the details of the favors he had called in and the promises he had made. He just gave him the results that he'd wanted. It was not the first time that Tyro had proved an invaluable friend.

"I'm still negotiating with the Central Posting Service about the Stop Comm order," Tyro said as Obi-Wan and Anakin greeted him in one of the Temple's small meeting rooms. "The good news is that the order has gone through. The bad news is that I don't know how long I can suppress the announcement of the arrest. But you might as well proceed to the Confiscation Station at the prison. You have a release for Slam's vehicle. It's an Ubrikkian star yacht."

Anakin whistled. "Sweet."

"All the data records, ID text docs, and wardrobes

are onboard," Tyro said. A small smile brightened his furry face. "I understand that Slam is a bit of a dandy."

Obi-Wan was more concerned with other matters. "Give us as much time as you can. It will take us a standard day to travel to Romin from the prison."

"You know I will do my best for you, my good friend," Tyro said. "You go into danger, and I wish you safety and success. The Svivreni do not say good-bye. We consider it bad luck. We say, *the journey begins, so go.*"

Tyro raised his hand, fingers spread, in the Svivreni gesture of good-bye. Obi-Wan did the same. Tyro then pressed his palm against Obi-Wan's. It was a gesture used by the Svivreni to those closest to them.

"So go," Tyro said softly, and left.

Mace's good-bye was not quite as fond as Tyro's. He agreed to the necessity of the plan, but he didn't approve of the rule bending.

"Just try not to alienate the entire Senate," he said. "In other words, succeed." He drew his robes together in dismissal. "May the Force be with you, and may I not hear from you until it's safely over."

The four Jedi had packed their gear and were streaking across the galaxy within hours.

At the Greylands Security Complex, they had no

trouble with the papers Tyro had supplied them with. They were given access to the Slams' ship.

The Ubrikkian star yacht was a light cruiser, built for quick getaways. Equipped with a hyperdrive, it carried no weapons except for two hidden proton torpedo shafts. It had also been modified to contain more secret compartments than Anakin had ever seen. Every time he thought he had found them all, he discovered another hidden within the various deck platings of the ship. The ship had been scanned by the authorities, in hopes of discovering the cache of crystalline vertex the gang had heisted on the Vuma job. No contraband had been found, and the rest of the gang's possessions had been searched and then left intact.

Ferus went through the computer files. The gang kept meticulous records and multiple ID docs for false identities. Siri found a device to override iris scans and, rolled into a tiny hidden compartment under the cockpit dash, a detailed analysis of the accounting practices of the Senate Relief Fund.

Ferus whistled under his breath. "I could be wrong, but I think they were planning to rob the Senate depository."

"That's a big job, even for the Slams," Obi-Wan said. "Good thing they landed in prison."

Anakin flipped further through the file. "This is just speculation. They didn't have a concrete plan."

"We'll go over the files in depth later," Siri said, her head in the Slams' personal wardrobe closet. "We'll have to be up on the latest criminal tech scams. There's a criminal gossip network. Our reputation will precede us. We have to *be* the Slams. Speaking of which . . ."

Siri pulled out a purple cloak made of veda cloth. It was embroidered around the collar with thick braiding in a bright shade of green. "For you, Slam," she said, handing it to Obi-Wan.

Obi-Wan eyed the garment. "Questionable taste, to say the least."

Siri winked at Anakin, but the face she turned to Obi-Wan was serious. "Tyro said that Slam is well known as a dandy. You have to wear it."

Obi-Wan's face was a study in distaste as he slipped on the ornate robe. Siri adjusted the elaborate collar so it framed his face. Anakin bit his lip. It was hard to keep his laughter inside.

Siri nodded thoughtfully. "Now you need some boots to match." She leaned over and pulled out a pair in red polished leather. "Here."

Obi-Wan took a step backward. "No . . ."

"Oh, for galaxy's sake, don't be such a stick-in-the-swamp." Siri tossed the boots at him. "You're impersonating a criminal. You have to dress like him. Don't you want to catch Zan Arbor?"

Siri turned her head slightly and winked at Anakin again. He turned away to hide his smile. Even Ferus looked as though he was suppressing a laugh.

Obi-Wan kicked off his travel boots and slipped on the soft leather boots. He turned to the large mirror on the inside of the closet door. "I really hate this," he groaned. "I look like a full-feathered idiot."

"I think you look . . . incredible," Siri said. But her mouth was twitching, as she couldn't keep it in any longer. She burst out into a peal of laughter.

It was impossible for Anakin and Ferus not to join in.

Obi-Wan raised an eyebrow at them. "So glad to amuse."

Then he reached into another closet. They heard the soft sound of rustling septsilk. Obi-Wan tossed a garment at Siri. It was made of a soft blue clinging material, and there wasn't much of it. "There you go, *Valadon*."

Siri looked at the piece of clothing. "Where's the rest of it?"

Obi-Wan grinned. "I'm afraid that's it."

"I'm not going to wear this." Holding it between her thumb and forefinger, Siri tossed the tiny garment away with distaste.

Obi-Wan's expression was bland as he retrieved it. "Don't be such a stick-in-the-swamp. Don't you want to catch Zan Arbor?"

Grimly, Siri pulled the robe over her tunic and leather leggings. Obi-Wan burst out laughing at the sight of the feminine, flowing garment haphazardly flung over Siri's rough clothes. "I don't think that's how you're supposed to wear it."

Siri gritted her teeth. "We're not on Romin yet."

Still chuckling, Obi-Wan reached into the closet and tossed out more conventional garments for Anakin and Ferus, dark tunics and trousers.

"Anakin, you'll be Waldo, and Ferus will be Ukiah," Obi-Wan said. "You fit the descriptions, roughly. Waldo is the security expert, and Ukiah is weapons and defense. Anakin, you'll need a headgear disguise, since you've seen Zan Arbor recently. I think that should be enough."

Obi-Wan pulled a half mask from his knapsack. "I got this from the med clinic at the Temple. It's used to knit synth-flesh together after an injury. We can tell people you were wounded in the escape, if they ask. Try it."

Anakin pulled on the mask. It fit over his forehead

and covered half his face, leaving his mouth and chin uncovered. There were holes cut for his eyes, with tinted lenses. It was made of a slippery fiber, and it felt cool against his skin.

He was glad to have something to hide behind. He remembered Zan Arbor's penetrating gaze, the sense that she wanted to explore his mind, figure out the essence of him. He didn't want Zan Arbor to know who he was. He didn't want to get close to the person who could create the Zone of Self-Containment. He still wasn't positive how the Zone was transmitted. He suspected it had been through water. That was something that Zan Arbor had perfected. Anakin never wanted to be under its influence again.

Was he wrong to think there had been some sort of connection between him and Zan Arbor? He hadn't told Obi-Wan about that. She had sensed there was something different about him. He had intrigued her. Even though he'd been in the Zone, he had sensed that this woman had made an impression on him he wouldn't forget. And he had made an impression on her. What if she recognized him again?

Obi-Wan was speaking, and Anakin wrenched his attention back to his Master. "I met Zan Arbor very briefly almost eighteen years ago. She won't recognize me."

Siri wrapped her utility belt around the soft blue

robe. "Question. What if we meet someone on Romin who's met the Slams before?"

"Not probable," Obi-Wan said. "The Slams operated in a different corner of the galaxy. Their reputation is big, but they didn't travel very far. It's a risk we'll have to take."

Obi-Wan's comlink signaled. It was Tyro, and Obi-Wan put him in holomode so the rest could view the communication.

Tyro flickered before them in miniature form. "I've received my answer from the authorities," he said. "I did my best, Obi-Wan. But I could persuade them to agree to keep the Slams' arrest secret for only three standard days. After that it will be posted on the HoloNet news. I'm sorry. You'll have to complete your mission in that time." Tyro looked worried. "Is three days enough?"

"Most likely not," Obi-Wan said. "But it will have to do."

CHAPTER FOUR

The Teda Landing Platform on Romin was high in the clouds above the capital city of Eliior. It was the only arrival station for the area. Nevertheless, it wasn't crowded. Anakin guided the ship down to the nearly empty platform.

"Not much business or tourism going on here," Obi-Wan observed. "The planet's economy runs on bribes paid to Teda."

"That means that the only one getting rich is Teda," Siri said.

Anakin released the ramp control. Siri strode down in front of Obi-Wan. Obi-Wan was amused by the contrast between Siri's purposeful, athletic stride and the lilac shimmersilk robe she now wore. It was tied with a rose-colored sash embroidered in delicate gold thread, but over the sash Siri had insisted on wearing her battered utility belt. Siri would do her best, she'd promised, but Obi-Wan had his doubts that she would be able to summon up Valadon's trademark flirtatiousness. It was good that this mission would be short.

"Look, that must be Zan Arbor's ship," Anakin murmured to Obi-Wan. Anakin and Ferus were wearing their minimal disguises, while Obi-Wan was nearly unrecognizable in his finery. All had managed to conceal their lightsabers except Siri, whose outfit was simply too revealing to cover much of anything. So Obi-Wan carried hers.

A sleek white ship was parked in a hangar nearby. Obi-Wan recognized the Luxe Flightwing. The nose of the cruiser was curved, the wings folded back like a bird's in flight. The ship's exterior was made out of a rare gleaming white ore.

A security officer met them at the bottom of the ramp. He was dressed in an ornate uniform with silver cords looping over his shoulders. The Romins were a species with golden skin and eyes. Their noses were flat, barely raised on their faces, and their mouths were wide and expressive.

"Welcome to Romin. Docs, if you please."

Obi-Wan handed over the ID docs. The officer perused them carefully.

"You have come to Romin for what purpose?"

"We would like to relocate here," Obi-Wan said.

The officer looked up. "There are procedures and waivers. We do not allow just anyone to be a citizen of Romin."

"We will be happy to follow all procedures," Obi-Wan said. "In the meantime, we would like to enter your beautiful city." He passed over a bundle of credits.

The officer slid them into his pocket in one practiced movement. "One moment."

The officer left with their four ID docs. He took them to a console and began entering the information.

"He plugged in our names and discovered that we're escaped criminals," Siri murmured as the officer's face changed. He looked up and gave them a quick glance. Then he spoke into his comlink.

They waited. The officer spoke, waited, spoke again. Then he put down the comlink but did not return to the visitors. The Jedi waited. They knew how to be patient. In a few moments, the officer's comlink signaled and he spoke into it again.

"We have to hope that Roy Teda's contacts are wide," Obi-Wan murmured. "He will know that there is a fortune in crystalline vertex out there, and that we know where it is."

When the officer returned to them, he was smiling broadly. "Forgive me if I failed to welcome you properly earlier. We are so busy here, you see."

"Of course," Obi-Wan said, waving his hand extravagantly and ignoring the empty spaceport.

"Due to your status as important guests, Great Leader Teda would like to extend a personal welcome," the officer said. "My name is Becka. With your kind permission, I am to escort you to his grand palace."

Becka led them to a large turbolift, which quickly brought them down to the planet's surface. A large, six-seat airspeeder was parked nearby. Becka indicated that they should board. He slid into the pilot seat. They glided out into moderate traffic on a wide boulevard.

"Eliior has no crime, as you will see," Becka said. "We have peace and prosperity here. Citizens have plenty of work and plenty of leisure time. Our gardens are renowned and our goods are the finest in the galaxy. I will take you by our best shopping street on the way to the palace and you will see."

"You are lucky to live on such a world," Siri said.

"We are lucky to have a leader such as Roy Teda," he replied. "He has created the great perfection around us." Just as Becka finished this statement, they drove by a battered security wall, hundreds of meters high. Security droids buzzed overhead.

"What is that?" Obi-Wan asked. He knew the answer, he was just interested in the official explanation. In a dictatorship, it rarely matched reality.

He'd been thoroughly briefed by Tyro. The city of Eliior was populated by the wealthy. The workers lived outside the city walls in concentric rings of hovels that grew progressively worse as their distance from the city increased. The wall was manned by guard droids and surveillance devices. The workers had to obtain passes in order to enter the city, and they needed a work reason for coming. Those inside the city rarely ventured outside its walls. If a trip was necessary, it was taken under heavy guard.

Becka made a quick turn down another wide boulevard lined with tall, leafy trees. "You mean the Cloudflower Wall. Some of our citizens prefer to live outside the city. There is beautiful countryside outside Eliior. The wall allows them to have the illusion that they live in wilderness. It is planted with cloudflower vines on the opposite side. Another great step of progression by Great Leader Teda! Truly, he is remarkable."

Just then they passed a large laserboard. In pulsing

light, the image of a noble-looking Romin appeared in profile. Words appeared in Basic:

WATCHING CARING PROTECTING

GREAT STEPS OF PROGRESSION

GREAT LEADER TEDA LOVES HIS PEOPLE

Becka beamed. "Now, here you will see examples of our excellent commerce and wonderful goods."

They rode down a street full of the exclusive shops that Becka had promised. They caught glimpses of luxurious goods arrayed in bright window displays. Becka slowed down and gestured to the shops with pride. Yet the street was nearly empty. There were hardly any customers in the stores.

"There's no one in the shops," Siri said.

"Not a traditional shopping day," Becka said. "Ah, now, here are our great residences."

Past the shops, the palaces began, made of stone and durasteel and glimpsed behind fortified walls. One by one, the grand structures appeared, framed by lush gardens and sparkling fountains.

"Many of our most substantial citizens live here," Becka explained. "One after the other, in luxurious and spacious villas. The boulevard ends at the grand palace complex of Great Leader Teda."

Soon a pair of ornate gates appeared ahead. Becka stopped the airspeeder at the security checkpoint and was admitted. The massive security gates opened. Ahead was a huge palace that sprawled over a lush landscape of flowers, trees, and shrubs. Flowering vines snaked around the trees and the high walls surrounding the compound. Their scent was heavy in the warm, humid air.

Becka pulled up in front of the main doors. "It was a pleasure to serve you," he said. Then, with an amiable wave, he took off.

The durasteel doors swung open. A short Romin man in flowing multicolored robes stood in the doorway. Obi-Wan recognized him immediately. He was surprised. Great Leader Teda had come to welcome them personally.

"Welcome to my world," Teda said, opening his arms wide. "So, what do you think of my Romin so far?"

Obi-Wan wondered what the flamboyant Slam would say. "Amazing!" he cried. He opened his arms wider than Teda's. "Incredible! We're overcome!"

"I am seeing that this is true by your faces!" Teda answered, beaming. "We Romins are so proud of our world that we are not surprised when visitors decide they must live here. On behalf of all Romins, I welcome you!"

Obi-Wan threw back his purple cloak and gave a short bow. "I am Slam. These are my associates, Valadon, Waldo, and Ukiah."

"And I am Great Leader Teda." Teda ignored Anakin and Ferus and headed directly for Siri. He slipped an arm through hers. "I have heard of your beauty, but words are nothing next to the reality of the realness of you. Your presence will only add to the beauty of our planet. You are prettier than a cloudflower." He stroked her arm with a finger.

The smile on Siri's face seemed fixed with a strong adhesive. Obi-Wan knew she was trying not to recoil from Teda's touch. "You're very kind," she purred admiringly.

He kept his face close to hers. He held up one chubby finger. "I speak only the most truthful truth in everything always. Remember that."

Siri lifted an eyebrow. "Truth in everything always? Then the reports are correct. You *are* a rare being."

Teda hesitated as he puzzled out what Siri meant. Then he laughed. "I'm hearing you now, and you have wit! You will return and have a long, lengthy lunch with me in my private dining room."

"Spoken like a true leader," Siri said through her tight smile. "You are used to being obeyed, I see. You issue invitations like orders."

Teda laughed again. He seemed delighted with everything Siri had to say. "Again, I am loving this. But unfortunately as a leader I have meetings, too many, always, I am telling you. You don't know the burden of my burdens. But I have them and I must attend to them." Reluctantly, he dropped Siri's arm. "But first, allow me to ease the difficulties of your first days on Romin. There is a villa nearby, small, but perfect. You will stay there. It is for sale, so it is unoccupied and empty right now. If you wish to buy it, you will buy it. If not, you will find something else equally as perfect. But for now, you may stay there without payment. My gift to you." His gaze lingered on Siri. "Beauty deserves beautiful surroundings."

"That is quite generous," Obi-Wan enthused. "We thank you." No doubt Teda wanted to keep tabs on them. It wasn't a problem. It was better that Teda think that he had them under his thumb.

"Now deputy Hansel will take care of you. For your listening pleasure, he will tell you a few things about the pleasurable pleasures of Romin." Teda gave Siri a meaningful look. "I will see you all again before too long. Or sooner, even."

The Great Leader turned abruptly and disappeared into the palace. Another Romin immediately appeared. He had obviously been waiting just out of sight.

"I am Hansel. Welcome to Romin. You have already seen something of the city of Eliior. While we enjoy a thriving economy, there are several charities close to the Great Leader's heart that are short of the funds they need to fully extend the great steps of progression. There is the Teda Institute for Children, for example. Also, the Teda Gallery of Horticultural Treasures of Romin. There are many native plants that are sadly in need of extra attention. I tell you this only so that you realize that Romin is not absolutely perfect in all areas. It is only correct that we do so. Great Leader Teda believes in truth in everything always."

"Yes, he already told us that," Siri said. "Naturally, it is true because he says it is, as he doesn't lie."

Hansel gave Siri a sharp look. Then he nodded politely. "Precisely."

Obi-Wan nudged her to be quiet. Insolence wasn't going to get them anywhere. It was obvious that Hansel was the official who had been sent to collect the bribe. Discreetly, Obi-Wan pulled out from beneath his layered robes a small bag stuffed with credits. "Please allow us to contribute to the needs of Romin's children," he said formally.

"Your generosity is astonishing. I will inform Great Leader Teda of it. And, in the days or weeks to come, I hope you will allow us to call upon you if we find there is an especially pressing need. . . ."

More bribes to come. Obi-Wan bowed his head. "Of course."

"Now, let me arrange transportation for you," Hansel said. "I understand that you will be occupying a villa in the secluded section."

"Thank you for your kind offer, but may we walk?" Obi-Wan asked, purposely modulating his voice. "If you give us directions, we'd like to stroll to our lodgings. It has been a long journey and before that we were . . . not able to get much exercise in the open air."

"Of course," Hansel said, not surprised in the least. "I will arrange for your things to be delivered. Just walk out the main gate and turn left. After five homes, you will see the villa. It is a golden color with a fountain in front. It has a black gate."

The Jedi walked away, several kilograms of credits lighter.

"I can't believe this," Ferus said. "The children of Romin will never see those credits."

"Not to mention the plants," Anakin said.

"This isn't a joke," Ferus said. "We just paid a fortune to a crook."

"We knew it was the only way to remain on Romin,"

Anakin said. "It does no good to question the decision now."

"I'm not questioning it," Ferus said defensively. "But I don't have to like it, either."

Obi-Wan listened to their bickering but decided not to interfere. Anakin and Ferus had to work out their mutual dislike on their own. Besides, he sympathized with Anakin. Ferus's self-righteousness could wear on the nerves. Paying the bribe had been a necessary step. It was useless to regret it.

"Teda doesn't seem very bright," Obi-Wan said, changing the subject. "I expected something different."

"He doesn't have to be bright, he just has to be a thug," Siri pointed out.

"It took us a day to get here, so we only have two days left," Obi-Wan said. "We should do some reconnaissance of Zan Arbor's house. It should be nearby, if we have the right coordinates. We'll do a quick survey of her security. Then we'd better get settled in the villa. No doubt Great Leader Teda will be keeping an eye on us."

A security officer opened the gate for them. They walked down the wide street, past the grand walls behind which palaces crouched, protected against invaders.

"I've never seen so many walls and gates in one city

before," Anakin observed. "I guess the criminals here have plenty of enemies."

"That's why they pay Teda so much. For refuge," Obi-Wan said. The four of them made their way down several long avenues, trying to keep a low profile. "Here is Zan Arbor's villa. Slow just a bit. See without looking."

Seeing without looking was a Jedi technique. Although they all appeared to be strolling by, each of them ticked off every security measure the villa had.

"The usual and then some," Siri said once they'd passed. "Security towers, armed windows, and doors."

"Infrared night sensors," Anakin added.

"Rooftop surveillance droids," Ferus said. "Plus random invisible energy fences on the grounds. This will be tough to break into."

"We'll take the easy way," Obi-Wan said.

"There's an easy way?" Ferus asked.

"There always is," Obi-Wan said. "We just walk in the front door."

CHAPTER FIVE

The Jedi arrived at their villa. It was modest, considering the neighborhood, but it was still several cuts above the places Obi-Wan and Anakin usually stayed on a mission. The sleep couches were deep and piled with luxurious coverlets. The reception rooms were large and sunny. A garden off the kitchen held flowering plants and flourishing vegetables and herbs.

"Are you sure we have to leave here in two days?" Anakin asked wonderingly.

Siri was completely uninterested in her surroundings. "They've created a paradise within the city walls, but it's an empty one. There is no economy to speak of. Did you see those stores? Expensive things to buy, but nobody except Teda and his confederates can afford them. And the workers live in misery right outside the walls." She shook her head. "How can anyone enjoy all this, knowing that?"

"It doesn't surprise me," Obi-Wan said. "They are glad they are inside the city walls, not outside. Now, we'd better get started." He turned to Anakin and Ferus. "Siri and I will make the first visit to Zan Arbor to gather information. In the meantime, you two should do some basic reconnaissance. Walk the streets. Have conversations. Note security, traffic patterns, and escape routes."

"Any specific objectives in mind?" Ferus asked.

"No," Obi-Wan said. "You never know what will turn out to be useful later."

"I've studied the maps of the city," Ferus said. "I'm sure I can plot possible escape routes or —"

Obi-Wan interrupted him curtly. "Maps are useful, but I learned something else from Qui-Gon. A map is not the territory. Go."

The two Padawans hurried off. Siri adjusted her utility belt. "I'm assuming you have a plan."

"Almost," Obi-Wan said. "Just follow my lead. Unless . . ."

"Unless?"

"Unless you'd rather stop off at Teda's for that

lunch," Obi-Wan teased. He ducked as an overstuffed pillow, lifted by the Force, flew straight at his head.

It was easy to get an audience with Jenna Zan Arbor. Obi-Wan merely announced at the front gate that Slam and Valadon wished to see her. Apparently, egomaniacal evil scientists and master thieves needed no introduction, for they were ushered inside immediately.

They were led to a room overlooking the gardens by a tall, hulking Phlog who was obviously a bodyguard. His gigantic hands pushed open a pair of double doors. As he walked through, his head barely cleared the doorway.

Zan Arbor sat in a chair perfectly positioned to backlight her bright hair and soften her features. She wore a simple silver gown with an azure belt.

Obi-Wan hadn't seen her in eighteen years. During that time he had changed much. He was taller. Older. Less surprised at the galaxy, and more rueful. Maybe sadder. On his occasional glimpses in a mirror, he saw the years on his face. It did not concern him; the fact that the years marked him was inevitable and right. Yet Zan Arbor looked almost unchanged from when he had known her. No doubt she consulted the best medical data in the galaxy to keep herself looking so well-preserved.

Obi-Wan bowed. "Thank you for seeing us."

Even while she smiled a greeting, Zan Arbor's green eyes ticked over him and Siri. "We new arrivals on Romin should stick together," she said. "Great Leader Teda has told me of your accomplishments. I was eager to make your acquaintance. Your reputation precedes you."

"As does yours," Obi-Wan complimented.

Zan Arbor waved at two ornate chairs placed in front of her. As Obi-Wan and Siri sat, she began to pour tea from a silver pot. The cups were made of translucent porcelain that Obi-Wan could see was among the finest the galaxy had to offer. Lovely urns and bowls were placed in a cabinet made of gleaming wood with fittings carved from rare stones. He looked around the beautifully appointed room. How had Zan Arbor managed to set herself up in such luxury so soon?

"And how are you finding Romin so far?" she asked, handing Siri a cup while seeming to notice every detail of her dress, down to her bare legs and her soft gold boots. Zan Arbor's lips pressed together in some kind of disapproval.

"We've only just arrived," Siri said. "But we are delighted to find it so pleasant and luxurious. Not to mention safe."

"Yes, you will not have to worry here," Zan Arbor said, handing a cup to Obi-Wan. "Great Leader Teda protects his friends. Romin is a perfect place to retire." She took a sip of tea, lowering her eyelids.

"Or not," Obi-Wan said.

Zan Arbor looked up.

"It is also," Obi-Wan said loudly, "a perfect place from which to do business."

Zan Arbor inclined her head. "That, too. Or so I hear."

"And we are far too young to retire," Siri said, following Obi-Wan's lead.

"As are you, I am sure," Obi-Wan said.

Carefully, Zan Arbor put her teacup down on a polished stone table. "Perhaps you should tell me why you've come."

"We've come to make the acquaintance of the finest scientific mind in the galaxy, it is true," Obi-Wan said, crossing his legs and smoothing out some of the feathers attached to his cloak. "We have also come to tempt you with an offer."

"I assure you, I am retired." Zan Arbor slid an errant blond hair back into her perfect coiffure. "But I am listening."

"We have a plan that I'm not at liberty to discuss fully," Obi-Wan continued. "It involves a great deal of wealth. A planetary treasury, in fact. You may have heard that we've had some success in that area. We're a modest bunch, but we're most confident we can build on that success." Obi-Wan smiled. Wouldn't Slam smile, at this moment? A con man would toot his own horn, but he would do it with a wink. He would seduce his listener.

Zan Arbor seemed to respond to his smile. She waved a hand, allowing him to proceed.

"We have the tech diagrams and a detailed way to get inside our target," Obi-Wan said. "We just need help with the guards. If we had an air delivery system that would slow down or incapacitate them for twenty minutes, we could raid the entire treasury."

Zan Arbor gave a tiny smile. "And so you came to me."

"Word has reached us of your experiments on Vanqor," Siri broke in. "An exciting development. You have the key to controlling minds. If you can control minds, you can control fortunes." She shrugged. "It's as simple as that."

"Or as complicated."

"We would arrange it so that your involvement would remain hidden," Siri continued. "We would take all the risks."

"You would be an equal partner, however," Obi-Wan said.

"We have the false ID docs ready," Siri said. "We can leave tomorrow. Tonight, if you wish. You could come aboard our ship, and we'd have you back here in two days. No one would even have to know you were gone."

Obi-Wan admired how Siri had picked up on his plan. Once they were in space, they could take her back to the prison planet. They would put her into custody without anyone getting hurt. Obi-Wan was hoping that her greed would be her undoing.

"A little effort for a great reward," Obi-Wan said. He flashed her a smile again, but this time she did not respond as before. He felt his heart sink.

"Why would I do this?" Zan Arbor waved a hand. "As you can see, I have everything I want. Every luxury is here. I live in a palace. I have the fastest ship in the galaxy at my disposal. What more do I need?"

"I have found," Obi-Wan said softly, "that there are needs, and there are wants. So the question is not what more do you need, but what more do you *want*?"

She raised an eyebrow, impressed with this despite herself. "Very clever. But I can supply my own wants." She pushed her tea tray away in dismissal. "Your little plan sounds intriguing. I wish you luck with it."

"I assure you, the rewards are greater than you can imagine," Obi-Wan said, trying again.

This seemed to amuse Zan Arbor greatly. "I doubt that." She gave a small laugh, as though to herself. "There is what I can imagine, and what actually lies ahead. I'm sorry to say that you must have more than this to tempt me. But don't take it personally. We cannot be collaborators, but we're going to be neighbors. Let us be friends as well."

Pasting a smile on his face, Obi-Wan thought for a moment. He refused to believe that Zan Arbor had truly retired. Why would she turn down a chance to raid a planetary treasury with very little risk to herself? Of course, she might be wary to commit to a plan with a gang she didn't know. Yet she had dismissed them quickly and then closed the door against any further exploration of working together.

Zan Arbor stood. "This has been lovely. I'm sure we'll meet again. Hue will see you out."

The same tall Phlog appeared. Zan Arbor disappeared through the doorway, leaving a waft of perfume behind.

"Charm him," Obi-Wan quickly whispered to Siri as he pretended to swipe a sweet from the tray.

She looked at Obi-Wan in disbelief. "Are you serious? He's a walking slab of muscle. It would be like charming a side of bantha meat."

"Valadon could do it," Obi-Wan pointed out.

He heard her breath hiss out between her teeth.

Obi-Wan hesitated by the tea table, pretending to finish his cup of tea. Siri sauntered across the room to Hue. Obi-Wan watched her over the rim of his cup.

He almost choked. The Siri he knew was gone. This Siri didn't stride across the room. She . . . *wafted*. Something happened with her hips and her legs and her hair. He wasn't sure what. He just knew that they moved differently. He just knew that whatever it was, it was female.

Siri locked her blue eyes on the Phlog's face. "You are one tall specimen, even for a Phlog," she said in a silky voice that was just as new to Obi-Wan. "You know, I always had a special thing for Phlogs. I feel so . . . protected when I'm around them."

Hue didn't blink, just kept dull dark eyes on Siri's face. "As long as we're on your side," he said sharply.

She smiled. "Is that a threat? Oooh. I'd better be on my best behavior."

Oooh? Did I just hear correctly? Obi-Wan couldn't believe it.

"You seem to be doing all right," the Phlog said.

"I've always wanted my very own bodyguard," Siri purred. "If you ever get tired of working here . . ."

"I'm tired of working here every day," Hue said. "But I work where the pay is. Know what I mean?"

"Very wise. I so admire a practical male," Siri cooed.

The slab of meat and muscle that was the Phlog looked suddenly as though his bones were made of crankcase oil. His hungry eyes followed Siri's every move as she enticed him farther out of the room and down the hallway.

"Could you take just the teeniest moment and let me peek into the gallery?" she asked him. "I'd love to see more of the house."

The Phlog followed Siri in her drifting shimmersilk as though he were attached by a string. Obi-Wan put down his teacup. The Phlog seemed smitten, but Obi-Wan doubted he had more than a minute.

He had been busy while chatting with Zan Arbor. He had practiced seeing without looking. He knew that the intricate and beautiful cabinetry concealed something. The joinery at the hinges and openings told him that.

He ran his fingers over the cabinet, calling on the Force to help his instinct, his vision, the very cells on his fingertips. He wished Anakin were here. Anakin's Force connection never failed to astonish him, even in his ease with inanimate objects. Once Anakin had told him that Soara Antana, the great Jedi fighter, had taught him how to let walls speak to him. Since then, Anakin had seemed to be able to judge the space between molecules as well as the objects the molecules made up.

Obi-Wan knew that somewhere in this house was evidence that Zan Arbor was planning something. It was an instinct, based on knowledge of her. Greed drove her, of course, but also her ego. She was not the type to retire.

And when she had said, *There is what I can imagine, and what actually lies ahead,* what had she meant? At first he'd thought that she was referring to the fact that he could have been overstating the rewards of his plan. But now he didn't think so. She was making a private reference to her own plans. Plans that would make his seem puny. That was the reason she had dismissed them.

Ah . . . there. Obi-Wan found the invisible seam. Another half second later, he found the catch. The cabinet opened silently, revealing a datapad, holofiles, comlinks — a concealed office.

He quickly pressed keys on the datapad. To his relief, not all the files were coded. He had so little time. He would have to start with the last file Zan Arbor had consulted. He keyed in the necessary steps. He, as well as Anakin, regularly kept up with the latest techniques from the tech expert at the Temple, Jedi Master Toma Hi'Ilani.

The holofile appeared in front of him. Communications from someone or some organization, merely identified with a random series of numbers that changed with every communication. A standard device for concealment.

He scanned it quickly. He could hear Siri's voice now, heading back toward the reception room, pitched just a bit louder to warn him. He read quickly.

Safe houses arranged . . .

Officials to bribe have been contacted . . .

A start date must be decided on with care . . .

Everything depends upon . . .

Obi-Wan whipped out his datapad and slipped in a miniature disk. It would take only a few seconds to copy the file.

"Oh, can't I just peek into the kitchen? You can't imagine how much I love to cook . . . no?" He could hear the playful petulance in Siri's voice, almost see her mouth pursing in a pout.

Ten seconds to go . . .

"Now, where did Slam go? I thought he was right behind us. He's probably still eating those sweets. . . ."

Five seconds . . .

"Oops, I dropped my scarf . . ."

Done.

Obi-Wan closed the holofile, slid the office shelf back into the cabinet, closed the false front, adjusted an urn, closed the cabinet, threw himself into a chair, and swept the sweets off the tray. He stuffed some down his tunic and two in his mouth just as they walked in the doors.

"Mmmfffphhh," he said to Siri.

She sighed. "I knew it! You ate them all! So rude, I have to apologize for him. We'll be going now."

Giving Hue a last flirtatious smile, Siri beckoned to Obi-Wan. Followed by the heavy tread of the Phlog, they accessed the front door and escaped into the sunlight.

"That had better be worth it," Siri said.

"It was," Obi-Wan said. "Zan Arbor is planning something. I made a copy of a work disk. Some of the files are coded. I can try to crack them back at the villa."

Siri shuddered. "I think that Phlog left fingerprints on my arm."

"*Oooh*," Obi-Wan teased.

Siri raised an eyebrow at him as they walked. "If you want to stay alive," she warned, "don't ever make that sound again."

CHAPTER SIX

They had seen the rich part of the city, so Anakin and Ferus searched out the scruffier streets, the places where commerce took place. Here there were small shops and businesses and warehouses, the engine that made the city run. It didn't take them long to realize how great the poverty of the workers was in contrast to the grand palaces in Teda's section of the city, and they weren't even outside the city walls yet.

Anakin's heart swelled with disgust. He had to concentrate to keep his breathing even. He had grown up with injustice. He had tasted it in his mouth like the sand that filled the air of Tatooine. The hatred he felt was bred in his bones.

"I hope one day Teda will pay for his crimes," Ferus said quietly. "He is robbing his citizens."

"He is killing them," Anakin said fiercely. "You don't know what it's like to be them. I do."

He had spoken angrily, dismissively. But Ferus didn't take offense. He merely nodded.

"Yes, you do," he agreed. "That is your great strength, Anakin."

His strength? Anakin had always thought of it as his weakness.

They were close to the wall now. They didn't want to get too close, for fear of alerting the security droids to their presence. Still, they wanted to observe the checkpoints. If access to their ship was suddenly cut off, would they be able to slip out of the city and disappear?

A shadow seemed to pass over him, although the bright sun was overhead. Anakin felt a Force surge, a warning. "Someone is tailing us," he told Ferus.

Ferus didn't turn. "I didn't see anyone."

"I feel it."

After a moment, Ferus spoke. "I feel it, too."

"Let's lead whoever it is on and then double back and see who it is," Anakin suggested.

They picked up their pace slightly, weaving in and out of alleys and staying in the shadows of the buildings. This close to the security wall, the section was run-down. Water ran down the gutters and pooled in the cracking pavement. Warehouses looked old and badly in need of repair. Occasionally they heard the scuttling of rodent creatures.

They turned a corner to a short block. Ahead, three dark alleys radiated out and were swallowed up in darkness. Perfect.

They didn't have to talk. They both began to run. They darted into the middle alley. Using cable launchers, they climbed to the top of the warehouse. From this vantage point they would see whoever was tailing them.

Below they saw a Romin cautiously move forward, gazing around with every step. He looked familiar.

"It's Hansel," Anakin said. "Come on."

He jumped to an overhang below, then down to the street directly in front of Hansel. Ferus followed a split second later.

Hansel gave a small yelp and jumped backward in fright.

"Looking for us?" Anakin asked.

Hansel tried to disguise his involuntary start of fear. He coughed and straightened his robes. "Ah, as a matter of fact, yes." He looked at them, his golden eyes speculative. "I did not expect to have to follow you here."

"Just doing a little sight-seeing," Ferus said.

"Let me assure both of you," Hansel said, "there are better sights to be seen. A curious choice, on your part."

"We got lost. What can we do for you?" Anakin asked.

"I am to deliver an invitation," Hansel said. "To Slam and Valadon. And the two of you, of course. Great Leader Teda is having a reception tomorrow evening and wishes you all to attend. Everyone will be there. You will meet many like yourselves."

"We accept, with pleasure," Ferus said.

"Be sure to give the message to Valadon," Hansel said. "Teda especially wishes her to be there."

"She wouldn't miss it," Anakin said.

"I will inform Great Leader Teda," Hansel said. "Now, no doubt you would like to continue your . . . sight-seeing."

He bowed and walked off, moving quickly.

"An invitation could've been sent to our villa. He suspects us of something," Ferus said.

"He just doesn't know what," Anakin said. "But we'll be gone before he figures it out. Well, I guess we should head back."

"I guess," Ferus said. "It's hard to know when we're done, isn't it? We had no clear objective. I like a clear objective. Otherwise I feel like I'm getting it wrong."

Anakin looked at him curiously as they began to walk. "I didn't think you ever thought you were wrong."

"I know that's what other Padawans think. It's because I try not to let it show. Don't you?"

Anakin snapped his mouth shut. Just when he thought he'd have a normal conversation with Ferus, he got caught up short again. Ferus was trying to trap him. He wanted him to admit weakness so he'd have something on him.

"This whole mission is unclear," Ferus went on, not realizing that Anakin had stiffened beside him. "I'll be happy when —"

The Force surged again. But this time it was too late. Caught up in their conversation and the relief of finding that it was only Hansel who had tailed them, they had let down their guard.

Their attackers came from behind on airspeeders. They used cables to knock Anakin and Ferus off their feet. Black hoods were thrown over their heads and tied shut.

Anakin rolled away from their attackers and rose to his feet in one fluid motion, ready to fight but not revealing his lightsaber. The hood was fastened in a way he couldn't figure out. That wasn't a problem. He had learned to fight in darkness; it was part of his Jedi training. But on Romin they were under strict orders not to use their lightsabers unless they absolutely had to. They had to retain their cover as part of the Slam gang.

Which meant they might learn more if they allowed themselves to be kidnapped. He could resist later. Anakin hoped that Ferus had come to the same conclusion.

He felt himself being shoved into a vehicle. Ferus hit the seat next to him.

"Any ideas?" Ferus grunted in a whisper.

"We might as well see who kidnapped us, and why," Anakin whispered back. "I think you just got your clear objective, Ferus."

A snort came from under Ferus's hood. "I would have preferred a different method. But thanks."

CHAPTER SEVEN

The hood was suddenly wrenched off Anakin's head. He took a deep breath of fresh air.

Only the air wasn't fresh. It was dank and murky, not much better than the hot, close air under the hood.

"That's right," a masculine voice said in a tone edged with sarcasm. "Take a deep breath of the wholesome country air of Teda Estates."

Anakin couldn't see who spoke. A bright light was in his eyes, and the rest of the room was in deep shadow. Ferus was next to him, his chin up as he tried to blink against the light. Anakin tensed, as if for a blow. He was ready to fight at any moment.

"Relax. We don't want to hurt you. We want to hire you. For stang's sake, B, turn off that light."

The light went out. Now the only light came from small windows cut in some sort of wooden structure. Water pooled on the hard-packed dirt floor. Anakin could hear the steady *drip, drip* of bad plumbing.

A Romin male emerged from the shadows. He was tall and slender. Energy seemed to be collected in his muscles and radiated out from his gestures and his pale eyes of light gold. The rest of the group stayed in the shadows.

"Sorry for the method," the tall Romin said. He pointed to Anakin's mask. "At least you are used to masks."

"Not really," Anakin said.

"We can't exactly issue nice personal invitations the way our Great Leader can. We needed to talk to you, and we needed to do it without any prying eyes or ears. We have a proposition."

"Who are you?" Ferus asked.

"My name is Joylin," the Romin answered. He brought a chair over by hooking his foot over the rail and dragging it. He sat astride, facing them. "I am the leader of the resistance on this planet. My face and name are well known to Teda. There's no need for concealment. My compatriots, however, are less well known and will remain hidden from you. The only thing you need to know is that there are many of us, and we do not all reside beyond the wall."

Which, Anakin reasoned, meant there were resistance members, or spies, in the city itself.

"What do you want with us?" Anakin asked. "We only just arrived on Romin."

"Exactly," Joylin said. "You do not yet have ties here. You have no friends, no loyalties. So you don't need to betray anyone to help us. Instead, you will do a straight trade. We will pay you, and you will help us. We are in need of your special skills."

"Why should we help you?" Ferus asked.

"Because you are thieves, and we will pay you," Joylin said impatiently. "And if you wish to remain on Romin, it would be a good idea to be on the winning side."

"The winning side? Are you going up against Teda and expecting to win?" Ferus looked around at the decaying structure. He was playing the game well, Anakin saw. A member of the Slams would naturally be incredulous and disdainful.

He decided to give Ferus the lead. In contrast, he would be the sympathetic one. They needed to find out as much as they could about this group.

"We will win because we have to win." Joylin spoke

without anger, without bravado. "What never fails to amuse me is when beings underestimate the power of desperation."

Ferus said nothing. Anakin waited.

Joylin spread his arms. "This is how we live on the other side of the wall. This is a typical dwelling. The only difference is, two or three families are usually crowded within its walls. Disease is rampant. Many of our children die before their second birthday. The ones who survive have no hope of getting better than a menial position, of traveling to the city once a day to rake a lawn, clean a sewer, fix a dataport."

"We have nothing to do with your troubles," Ferus said.

"Ah, of course not. You just take advantage of them. You accept the offer of a tyrant for a hideout."

Anakin broke in. "Are you going to insult us or offer us a job?"

A strained smile creased Joylin's face. "Right. Okay, here is the offer. We'll pay double your going rate for stealing a certain piece of information at Teda's villa. We've been waiting for the right events to coincide, and at last they have. Teda is giving a big reception, and thieves with special skills have arrived on Romin."

"You want us to steal from *Teda*?" Ferus blustered. "Forget it!"

"What do you want us to steal?" Anakin asked quickly.

"A small item from his private office," Joylin said. "It contains information that will guarantee our success. Within a short time we will be able to take over the government. Which means you will be the only group of criminals allowed to stay on Romin. Each member of your gang will be given lifetime citizenship. As long as you don't break Romin's laws, you'll be welcome here."

"Keep talking," Anakin said. "We need more to take back to our boss."

"We happen to know that in Teda's study there is a list of codes that control the security gates to all official government offices and residences, as well as the sheltered criminals."

"Wait a minute." Anakin pretended not to understand. "Are you telling us that Teda has access to everyone's personal security?"

Joylin nodded. "It's not a secret. Most of them accept it as the price for staying on Romin. He says he needs to be able to lock down the palace neighborhood in case of unrest."

"How do you know he has the codes in his residence?" Ferus asked.

"You will have to trust that our information is accurate," Joylin said. "We have someone on the inside."

"Can that someone help us get into the palace?" Anakin asked.

"No," Joylin said. "We can't compromise our agents. Besides, you don't need help. You have an invitation to a reception, don't you? That is the night we want you to steal the codes."

"How do you know we've been invited?" Ferus challenged.

"We know," Joylin said. "I told you, there are many of us. Enough to ensure success, if we strike quickly and decisively."

Anakin looked at Ferus. It was strange. He didn't even like Ferus, but now that they were together in this situation, he could read him without speaking. They were in tune. They needed to get more information. To do that, they had to draw Joylin out. They would do it in tandem.

Ferus shook his head. "I'm sorry, but we have to refuse."

Joylin's face tightened. "Can you tell me your objections?"

"Delighted," Ferus said. "You're asking us to stake our future on a bet. That normally wouldn't be a problem. We risk our future all the time. But the reason we're successful is that we're careful. You're asking us

64

to make a powerful man our enemy, just when he's offered us safe refuge."

"This is not a safe refuge," Joylin argued. "I assure you, your protection will disappear. Unless you throw your support to the ultimate winners."

"But if we don't steal the codes, you have no chance," Ferus argued back.

"There will still be a revolt," Joylin said. "It just won't be bloodless. You will be in more danger the other way, because I won't protect you."

Ferus started to say something, but Anakin broke in. It was time to draw Joylin in. Sometimes Anakin wasn't sure if it was the Force or his instincts, but he was getting better at seeing inside beings, sensing their fears and motivations. Joylin might be sitting casually, but Anakin could feel his urgency. And underneath the urgency, fear. The Slams could be his last chance.

"We still need more information," Anakin said carefully. "Surely you can see that we can't simply take your word for what you say."

"I'm hardly about to compromise the safety of those in the resistance just to reassure you," Joylin said.

"We're not asking you to reveal identities or secrets," Anakin told him. "But what makes you think you can overthrow Teda so easily? When are you going to do it? What will happen when you do? You are asking us to trust you. You must trust us. We are taking a risk for you. You must do the same."

Joylin hesitated. He looked at both of them. He did not glance behind at the watching, shadowy group.

It's his decision, Anakin thought. *He's the boss.*

"The revolt is to be the night of the reception," Joylin said.

Someone behind him gasped. Someone else said, "No!"

Joylin only half turned. "We must tell them! Once they know, they will help us." He turned back to Anakin and Ferus. "We'll start by disrupting communication systems — just some low-level interference at first. We have already infiltrated Teda's Security Management Control. We have one chance to sabotage the CIP controls for the droid army that Teda uses to control the city and guard the wall. If we strike that blow simultaneously with the capture of all government officials and Teda himself, we can win without bloodshed. We'll simply lock the officials and their personal troops inside their houses. Without the officials, without the droid army, we can take over."

Ferus and Anakin didn't say anything for a moment.

"You can assure us that the droid army will be in your control?" Ferus asked.

"Yes."

"You will pay us double the rate?" Anakin asked. He named the figure.

"We have it. It has taken years," Joylin said. "Every family, every individual, has gone without in order to feed our treasury."

"We're not interested in how you got it," Ferus said with a wave of his hand. "But we need to assure for ourselves that you *do* have it. Half before, half after the revolt."

"Agreed," Joylin said.

"We need more detailed information on where we can find the codes," Anakin said, all business now.

"All you have to do is get beyond the guards. I understand that you are somewhat expert at that."

Anakin and Ferus nodded. "We must take this back to Slam and Valadon," Anakin said. "We will need a way to contact you."

"We will be contacting you tomorrow morning," Joylin said. "Don't look for us. We'll be there. Now, I'll escort you as far as the wall. I'm sure you were told it is planted with cloudflower vines. It may not surprise you to find that isn't the case. Like peace and justice on Romin, the name of the wall is just an illusion."

Anakin and Ferus stood. "Just one more thing," Anakin said.

Joylin looked at him. With a deal so close to being made, his anxiety had increased. Anakin could feel it humming like a charge in the air.

"We are interested in one of the residents here," Anakin continued casually. "A scientist named Jenna Zan Arbor. You must guarantee safe passage for her off-planet. We will arrange transportation."

Ferus's eyes flickered with surprise at Anakin's proposal. *What if Joylin backed out?* Anakin knew he wouldn't. Joylin was good at concealment. It was most likely a way of life for him. But Anakin could feel his hunger.

If the coup went through as planned, Zan Arbor would be desperate to get away. The Slams could offer her a way out. With the collapse of Teda, her security would crumble. She would need help.

"That is not a problem," Joylin said. "As long as you are in."

CHAPTER EIGHT

"He tells us there is no risk, but of course there is risk," Ferus said later that evening. Obi-Wan, Siri, Anakin, and Ferus had eaten a meal around a tiled table in a small, lovely room overlooking the garden. They were careful to speak of nothing of consequence during the meal. They had to assume that the villa had listening devices. But afterward they had gone into the garden. Then they had continued the discussion that had begun when Anakin and Ferus had first returned to the villa and beckoned to Obi-Wan and Siri to come outside.

"It's a risk worth taking," Anakin said. Obi-Wan was glad to hear that there was not the usual edge in his voice. Anakin was disagreeing with Ferus. That was usual. But he was doing it without resentment. That was good.

Their adventure together had brought Anakin and Ferus closer. Obi-Wan didn't delude himself that they were friends. But he did think something had changed.

He kept only half his attention on the argument, letting the words of the others wash over him. With the other half of his mind, he was flipping through the holofile he'd copied at Zan Arbor's. He had read every word of the uncoded files, enough to tell that she was planning a new operation, this time with partners. *Everything depends upon secrecy and speed.*

The rest of the files were coded, and he had tried the most difficult formulas he knew to break the code. He had called for help from the Temple and had worked with one of their codebreakers. No luck.

Siri was hanging back, letting the two apprentices discuss the situation. It was good for them to do so, and they were doing it well.

"If we help them, we will be actively supporting an overthrow of power on a planet," Ferus said. "We have no Senate authorization to do so."

"We are not the ones overthrowing Teda," Anakin objected. "And the citizens of Romin are suffering. If we can help them and achieve our mission, why shouldn't we?"

"Because it can get out of control," Ferus argued. "Joylin can surprise us. We don't know anything about this resistance movement. We don't know who they are or what they want, apart from overthrowing Teda."

"They are an established resistance group," Siri broke in. "I contacted Jocasta Nu to ask about them. They have been put down in brutal reprisals, but the movement has been growing steadily in response to Teda's crackdowns. Madame Nu believes there may be support within Teda's government as well. They, too, are tired of living in fear. Teda's prisons are notorious and overcrowded, and you earn a harsh sentence if you displease him. She would not be surprised if many in the army desert. Many of them have families who live outside the wall. They know firsthand the misery and poverty there."

"You see?" Anakin said. "Joylin and his group are fighting for justice. As we are. We can help them *and* bring Zan Arbor back to the prison world. You're making this complicated, Ferus. It isn't."

I'm making this too complicated, Obi-Wan thought. *It isn't.*

He thought for a moment, remembering Zan Arbor's primary obsession. He keyed it in as a password: The Force.

The files opened like the motion-sensor doors at the Warm Welcome Inn on Coruscant. One after the other they flashed *code accepted.* Obi-Wan accessed the first file. The voices of the others faded as he began to scroll through the information.

A chill ran over him, even though the night was warm. The letters pulsed before his eyes. A name he hadn't expected to see. Yet shouldn't he have been prepared for it? Wouldn't Zan Arbor naturally gravitate toward the most powerful criminal in the galaxy, one with the wealth and organization to help her with any scheme she might devise? Or had he contacted her, the one scientist brilliant and amoral enough to join with him? Didn't they share the obsession with the Force and how it worked?

Granta Omega.

A copy of a message, a profuse thank you from Zan Arbor for Omega's hosting of their first meeting.

A quick message saying she had to evacuate the Vanqor system and would be in touch.

A confirmation of their next meeting, in which she alluded to their shared interest in the Force.

Another letter, promising to destroy all written records of their correspondence, a promise that of course she had not kept, possibly as security.

Obi-Wan flipped through the next file. The two of them were careful. They never said exactly what they were planning. Yet it was clear the operation would take place on a large planet in the Core. It would net them not only wealth, but influence.

Siri's voice broke through his thoughts.

"I've listened to you both very carefully, as has Obi-Wan," she said, shooting him a chastising look, for it was clear to her that he hadn't been paying attention in the least. "You both make valid points. We must make a decision, however. I think we should go ahead and help Joylin's group. Obi-Wan?"

"There is another factor we must consider," Obi-Wan said. "These files indicate that Zan Arbor is in league with Granta Omega."

"Omega!" Anakin exclaimed in surprise.

Siri and Ferus suddenly became grave. They all knew that these two powerful criminal minds could do more than double the damage if they became partners.

Obi-Wan met Siri's eyes. She nodded.

"We are going to help the resistance," Obi-Wan said. "We will take the risk. We need to get Zan Arbor off this planet. We only have tomorrow before our cover could be blown. The best chance we have is if she thinks her safety here is compromised. We will offer her a way out. She will have to take it. There is only one thing."

Siri cocked an eyebrow at him. He noted that she

looked her old self, in her tunic and leggings. It was as if the sight of her in her drifting shimmersilk had been an apparition.

"We might not want to take her to the prison planet," he continued. "If we do it right, she could lead us to Omega himself."

"We would have to contact Mace," Siri said.

Obi-Wan nodded. "I think he would agree. I'll contact him tonight. It will help us if he can start working on Senate approval for us to help the revolt. But it won't come in time."

Suddenly, their mission had grown in importance. Granta Omega could be within their grasp again. This time, Obi-Wan would not lose him.

"We can decide where to take Zan Arbor another time," Obi-Wan said. "But we should all agree that if we can track Omega through her, we will."

"I agree," Siri said quietly.

"I do, too," Anakin said.

Ferus nodded.

"Now let's all get some sleep," Obi-Wan said.

Nevertheless, he knew he would not.

Romin had only one moon, but it was a large, luminous satellite. That night its light seemed enormous to Obi-Wan. It kept him from the sleep he tried vainly to reach.

At last he gave up. He rose from his sleep couch, opened the double doors to the stone patio outside, and walked into the fragrant garden. The air felt heavy. The heat from the day had lingered. Obi-Wan moved among the flowering shrubs. He found the play of moonlight on the glossy leaves more calming than lying on his sleep couch, waiting to feel drowsy. He would let the sights and sounds around him lull him into a kind of relaxation that he hoped would be as restorative as sleep.

He followed a path crowded with bushes that suddenly opened into a small grassy clearing. Ferus sat cross-legged in the middle of the clearing, his eyes closed. Obi-Wan stopped, not wishing to disturb him.

He was turning to go back to the house when Ferus spoke.

"You couldn't sleep either, Master Kenobi?"

Obi-Wan moved forward. He sat on the grass next to Ferus. It was slightly damp and smelled sweet.

"There are many questions on my mind," Obi-Wan said. "Sleep won't come."

"We face a great enemy," Ferus said. "And now we find that she's met with a greater one."

"Exactly."

"And that is why you and my Master made your decision this evening," Ferus said.

"You don't agree." Obi-Wan spoke carefully.

"I don't disagree," Ferus said. "I recognize that I don't have the experience to refute what you say."

Obi-Wan stifled a sigh. He could see why Anakin had a hard time with Ferus. Ferus always said the correct thing. Obi-Wan preferred the spontaneity of his own apprentice.

"I sense your impatience," Ferus went on. "You think I only say the correct thing just to impress you or my Master."

"I don't think that," Obi-Wan said. "Well, not exactly."

"Can I help it if the Jedi wisdom I have learned by rote speaks to my heart?" Ferus asked. "I don't say things because they will please you. I say them because I feel they are true. It's always been that way, from my earliest memory of the Temple. When I was taught, it was as though I already knew. Every Jedi lesson seemed to fit a groove inside my mind that had already been worn. It was why learning was so easy for me."

"You have a great connection to the Force," Obi-Wan said. "No doubt that is why."

"So does Anakin," Ferus pointed out. "Far greater

than mine. I can see that. Yet he did not have the problems I did at the Temple. He has made great friends there."

Obi-Wan was surprised. "But you were popular in your class. Everyone looked up to you."

"Yes, I was the one whom everybody liked, but whom nobody wanted to talk to. I was welcome at every table in the eating areas, but not invited to any particular one. Everyone was my friend, but nobody was my particular friend." Ferus picked some grass and let it fall idly through his fingers. "I've heard the names they call me. A tunic stuffed with feathers and the Force. The ruler of Planet Dull."

Obi-Wan frowned. He had not known these things.

Ferus waved a hand. "It's all right. It's all true, isn't it? I've never been able to joke like the others. I know I can be pompous, too correct. I never learned how to tease the other students. They came to me for help with their studies, they looked to me for answers, but no one wanted to be my friend. Not my true friend, the way Anakin has Tru Veld and Darra."

Was it a trick of the moonlight, or did Ferus suddenly look younger than his years? Usually, he looked much older. His noble features and the streak of gold in his dark hair had given him a look of maturity early on.

But now he looked uncertain, questioning. Young.

"You will find friendships later in life," Obi-Wan said, after a pause. "Friendships are hard to maintain for the Jedi. It is why we treasure them. Let go of your longing, and what you want will come."

"Or else I am meant to stay the way I am," Ferus said. "I wish I had what Anakin has. His connection to the Force is strong, yet he also connects to beings very strongly."

"Yes," Obi-Wan agreed. "I've seen this. It's something Qui-Gon Jinn had, too."

"I know that Anakin will never be my friend. He knows I fear for him. I give him warnings when I know I shouldn't, when I know it's none of my business. So he resents me. I thought in the beginning . . . since I was a little older . . . that I could tell him things that other students couldn't. It's just I see things a fellow student would see."

Here it was. Ferus had been leading to this. He wanted to tell him something. Obi-Wan felt impatient with him, but he calmed the impulse. He felt protective of Anakin. Ferus didn't understand him. He had always been the correct student, the one who did everything right. He could not begin to know the fears and regrets Anakin had to deal with.

"And what do you see, Ferus?"

"I fear for him," Ferus said quietly. "To admire him and feel fear for him at the same time didn't make sense to me. It took me a long time to understand *why* I feared for him. I wanted to be sure there was no envy in it."

"Do you envy him?" Obi-Wan asked.

"I suppose all the students do, in a way," Ferus said. "He is the Chosen One. But what worries me is his will." Ferus hesitated. "His power is so great that he thinks his judgment is as well. You saw his arguments tonight. He sees something is right, so therefore he must do it. He argues against you without hearing you. He thinks he can change situations, beings. Maybe he can't do it alone, not yet. But someday he will. Should we trust someone who always believes he speaks with the voice of absolute right?"

That is it, Obi-Wan thought. *That is what I see.* What surprised him was that it was coming out of the mouth of one of Anakin's peers, a boy only a year or two older than Anakin, someone who had only been on a couple of missions with him.

Ferus is always watching me, Anakin had told Obi-Wan resentfully.

And so Ferus was. But Ferus's mature judgment surprised Obi-Wan. Surprised him and irritated him, he had to admit. Ferus did not allow for the goodness of Anakin's heart. He did not see how hard Anakin tried. He did not know that Anakin questioned himself all the time.

"You are very observant, Ferus, but you must accept that I know him better than you," Obi-Wan said carefully. "Anakin can be arrogant. I know that. But he is also learning and growing. He is respectful of his great power. He does not abuse it. He is younger than you, but he has seen much injustice, many terrible things. I do not think it so wrong that he wants to change things. You must understand that it isn't ambition that drives him. It is compassion."

Ferus nodded slowly. "I will think about what you said." He stood. "Please know that I say these things only because he is the Chosen One, and the stakes are so high. Good night, Master Kenobi."

"Good night," Obi-Wan said.

He could have said more, but it wasn't appropriate to debate Anakin's character with another apprentice. He would have to sift through Ferus's words and ponder them. He would have to let go of his impulse to protect Anakin and search for the truth in what Ferus had said. Ferus had touched on his own fears, and he needed to think about that.

He breathed in the night air. *Not tonight,* he decided. He valued his new confidence in Anakin. He needed to guard it. He needed to forget what he feared, just for a little while longer. He wanted to treasure what he had.

CHAPTER NINE

They could see the lights and hear the noise before they even passed through the security check. Teda's villa was ablaze with colored laserlights. Tableaus of different worlds renowned for their natural beauty were arranged on the grounds. Each scene was a small-scale replica of that world's greatest landmarks.

"Dremulae, Off-Canau, Xagobah, Belazura," Ferus said, naming the worlds as they walked by. Native flowers from each of the worlds wafted delicate scents into the air. Servers walked about with repulsorlift trays carrying an array of native foods.

The biggest tableau was for Romin itself. A small-scale replica of Eliior had been built out of massed flowers. There were models of Teda Park, the Teda Institute for Advanced Study, and the Roy Teda Colored Fountain of Lights. At the party, the Cloudflower Wall was actually fashioned out of cloudflowers. To reach the Romin display, the guests walked under a large arch upon which laserlights spelled out the message THE MOST BEAUTIFUL WORLD OF ALL WORLDS.

The party was crowded with Romins and others who lived in the palace district, all dressed in their finest. The Jedi had likewise worn the rich robes of the Slams, wanting to blend in. Siri had chosen a shimmersilk sleeveless tunic in colors that shifted from blue to green to silver as she moved, the colors of the sea as the day moved from dawn to twilight. She had refused to wear the matching green slippers, however, pulling on her travel boots instead.

"Just in case I have to run from Teda," she said.

Obi-Wan felt awkward wearing a heavy septsilk tunic in one of the purple shades that Slam was so fond of. It was heavy and stiff, embroidered with gold thread and tiny jewels. Anakin and Ferus had dressed in less elaborate fashion, pulling on simple tunics in navy and gold.

"The security is tight," Obi-Wan said as his eyes noted the many agents, some overt and some secret, in the throng.

"Just what we'd expect," Siri said. "Joylin told us that the door to his study won't be armed."

"Let's hope he's right. But first, we'd better say hello to our host."

"Do we have to?" Siri groaned.

It wasn't easy to find Teda in the crush of the crowd. They bumped into Becka, the officer who had checked them in at the spaceport. He greeted them happily, with a flushed face and outstretched arms.

"My new arrivals! How glad I am that you are here! Have you tried the delicacies from the different worlds? Can I get you a plate of food?"

"We're looking for Great Leader Teda," Obi-Wan said. "We'd like to thank him for his hospitality."

"I saw him in the house," Becka said. "He checks every detail. How lucky we are to have such a leader! Let me take you to him."

Becka led them quickly through the throng. The grand palace was decorated as lavishly as the grounds. Banks of flowers were massed in the hallways. Tables with punch and food were set up in every corner. Different bands of musicians played in different rooms, so that the hallways were a mass of noise in which one couldn't pick out a single tune. It was as though one party wasn't enough for Teda. He had to pile ten parties on top of one another to make one big extravaganza. There was so much food and drink and music and so many flowers that guests lurched about in a daze, as though they were droids with overloaded sensors.

They saw Teda's broad back ahead. Obi-Wan heard his voice above the crowd. He was berating a server in a white tunic.

"You were instructed not to serve the dameapple turnovers until *after* the skewered runis!" he said. He wasn't shouting, but the words were hissed in such white-hot anger that they seemed charged with turbo power.

The server's face now matched his tunic. "I was told in the kitchen —"

With a casualness that shocked Obi-Wan to the core, Teda lifted a small electrojabber and struck a hard blow against the server's knees. The server crumpled, eyes wide. He knew better than to cry out against the pain.

Becka, too, went pale.

"Our leader, so forceful, so strong," he murmured. "How lucky we are to have him." Becka backed away and disappeared into the crowd.

Obi-Wan didn't blame him. In a world ruled by an unpredictable tyrant, citizens had to rely on an instinct for flight to stay healthy.

Teda turned. Obi-Wan was surprised again. There was no sign of anger on his face, just a slight tautness around his mouth. It was as if the rage had never existed.

He held out his arms to the Jedi. "Welcome, Slams! Now the party can begin! Have you eaten? Have you met new friends?" He came forward and put his arms through Obi-Wan's and Siri's. It took an effort for Obi-Wan to allow it. He knew Siri felt the same.

Other servers had rushed to help their fallen comrade. They half carried, half dragged him toward the kitchens.

"The theme of the party is paradise," Teda continued. "I've gathered all the best of the galaxy for the citizens of Romin. Even though the best of the best is already here, ha-ha!"

Not all the citizens. Only the ones that you favor, Obi-Wan thought as he said, smiling politely, "Thank you for inviting us."

Teda withdrew his arms from theirs. "Now, don't get stuck talking to an old man like me. Go enjoy yourselves!" He smiled at Siri meaningfully. "I will check on you later."

Teda hurried over to greet some new arrivals.

"I can't believe what I just saw," Ferus said. "He hit that server with an electrojabber with no more emotion than if he were swatting a squeeterfly."

"And you doubt that we are doing the right thing in helping the revolt?" Anakin asked.

Siri changed the subject. "Ferus and I will check out the security on the target," she said.

"I'll check out the perimeter of the palace," Anakin said. "We should map out an escape route just in case. Let's remember: We don't have much time."

That left Obi-Wan without much to do. Joylin had told him that he could not attempt a theft of the codes until after midnight. He had time to kill.

He moved through the crowd, hoping for a glimpse of Jenna Zan Arbor. He didn't know if he would approach her, but he wanted to keep tabs on her, just the same. He wondered what her relations with Teda were. It seemed from the files he'd read that Teda had invited her to come to Romin after she was forced to flee Vanqor. Was there a connection to Omega? Had Omega pressured Teda to invite Zan Arbor?

Obi-Wan drifted toward a table with assorted drinks. He chose a glass of juice made from the native quintberry fruit of Romin. He took a sip and made a face. It was very sweet.

Joylin had given him explicit instructions on where to find the codes and where the security triggers would be. Joylin was counting on Slam's conning expertise to get past the guards. Obi-Wan would simply use the Force. If he was lucky, he could be back in the villa very soon after the theft. But if the revolt really did take place that night, he would go another night without sleep.

Suddenly, his senses went on alert. A young man with a tired, handsome face was heading toward the drinks table.

Obi-Wan knew that face from text docs he had studied. He did not need the Force to warn him.

He looked around. There was nowhere to go.

"Hey, a fellow thirsty traveler," the man said to Obi-Wan, pouring a glass of juice. "Some party, huh? I'm Slam."

CHAPTER TEN

Obi-Wan thought quickly. By the open, unguarded look on Slam's face, he doubted that Slam knew someone was impersonating him.

"I've only just arrived," Slam said in an amiable way, leaning back against the bar and sipping his juice. He made a face. "Whoa, sweet. Just like my landing spot."

"So you like Romin already?" Obi-Wan asked.

Slam gave a half smile. "Let's say it likes me. The rest of the galaxy isn't too . . . welcoming. Hey, nice tunic."

If Slam had noticed that Obi-Wan hadn't given his name, it clearly didn't concern him. Obi-Wan imagined that in Slam's universe, many beings did not use names or discuss their occupations.

"I just got here yesterday myself," Obi-Wan said.

Slam waved a glass of juice at the throng. "Interesting party."

"Paradise, I hear," Obi-Wan said. "At least, that's the theme."

Slam laughed. "Well, it looks like paradise to me. It was a rough trip for me and my friends."

So his gang is here, too. They must have escaped again. Tyro told us that escapes are common now. I have to warn the others.

"I'm supposed to meet Teda tonight. And pay the usual bribes, I'm sure things seemed a bit disorganized at the landing platform. They were having trouble with comm transmissions."

Joylin, Obi-Wan realized. They had started to disrupt communications.

"We never got a chance to get our official entry docs," Slam continued. "So, what's the Great Leader like?"

Obi-Wan spoke lightly. "Oh, he's just your average everyday dictator."

"So I hear. But for beings like me, your average everyday dictator comes in handy."

"A word to the wise, though," Obi-Wan said casually. "I wouldn't try to meet him tonight. He's in a bad mood. I just saw him use an electrojabber on a waiter."

Slam winced. "Ouch. Thanks for the tip. Well, I think I'll try the food tables instead, then."

The real Slam moved off.

Obi-Wan glanced at his chrono. He had barely ten minutes before he had to lift the codes. He had to find the others. The party was over for the Jedi.

Ferus spoke quietly, incredulously, to Anakin. "Are you seeing what I'm seeing?"

Anakin gulped. "I think so."

"She's . . . *flirting.*"

"It looks like it."

"She's . . . *flattering* people."

"Yes."

"And she's . . . *smiling.*"

"It's not just that she's smiling," Anakin added, in the interest of accuracy. "She's *gushing.*"

Siri stood in the middle of a group of admirers. Someone had tucked a bright red flower behind one of her ears, and, as Ferus had hissed to Anakin in a fierce undertone, *Siri left it there!* Anakin watched as she placed a hand on a security officer's coat sleeve and leaned over to whisper in his ear. He leaned back and roared with laughter.

Whoever would have believed, Anakin thought in amazement, *that Siri Tachi could be charming?*

It was a night of wonders. His own Master was wearing a cloak with jeweled embroidery and pretending to love parties.

He had to laugh at the look on Ferus's face. After a moment, Ferus broke down and grinned, too. "I think Siri is just pretending to hate this," he said. "I think she's enjoying herself."

"I think you're right," Anakin said. He glanced at his chrono. "We have about seven minutes. We should get into position."

Just as he said it, Siri said one last remark that caused the group of males around her to laugh uproariously. Then she turned away graciously. She joined Anakin and Ferus a moment later.

"I've discovered something," she said. "Charm is exhausting. And something else. Flattery works. I've learned some things. Half the surveillance droids are fakes. Every day more officers are deserting the army. They haven't been paid in months. Teda's running out of wealth. He can't afford to prop up his government much longer, so he's looking for income wherever he can find it. In the meantime, he's cutting back."

"I've found a way out if we have to escape," Anakin said. "It would be difficult, but not impossible. There's a part of the wall that's less heavily guarded. It's behind a dense thicket of bushes with bright flowers and thorns a meter long. We could use the Force to jump over the thicket, then activate cable launchers in midair, scale the wall, and take out droids with our lightsabers as we climb. I'm not sure what we'll find on the other side. Guards are no doubt patrolling outside the palace as well."

"All in all, we just have to hope Obi-Wan doesn't get caught," Siri said.

"I'll do my best," Obi-Wan said as he came up behind her. "But in the meantime, we have another problem. The Slam gang is here. The real one."

"That's not good news," Siri said. "Does Teda know?"

"Not yet. There's interference in the comm systems. Joylin's work, no doubt. I tried to give Slam a warning about approaching him tonight. But I doubt it will keep them apart for long. Teda is making the rounds."

Siri frowned. "Time just ran out."

"This is all the more reason to help with the revolt," Anakin said. "If it's successful, we won't have to worry about Teda *or* the Slams."

"Still, we can't take a risk for all of us," Obi-Wan said. "This party suddenly got very small. The three of you should head back to the villa and prepare for a quick departure with Zan Arbor. I'll steal the codes, meet up with Joylin, and join you at the villa."

Anakin shook his head. "I'm not leaving you here, Master."

"Yes, you are, because I'm ordering you to," Obi-Wan said. "Remember, my young apprentice. The mission is first."

Obi-Wan put a hand on Anakin's shoulder briefly. The gesture told Anakin that he appreciated his support, but his decision was firm.

But Anakin still didn't want to go.

"Obi-Wan is right," Siri said. "But nevertheless, we are not leaving."

Obi-Wan looked annoyed. "Siri, I don't have time to argue."

"Precisely. You need us to remain. We'll watch out for the Slams. As soon as you get the codes, we'll all go."

"I don't like this," Obi-Wan said.

Siri was adamant. "Too bad."

Only a slight pressing of his lips showed Obi-Wan's displeasure. He turned abruptly and disappeared into the crowd.

Ferus let out a breath. "Whatever happened to flattery to get what you want?"

"Flattery doesn't work on Obi-Wan," Siri said. "Speaking of which, I'll track down Teda. I'll keep him away from the Slams. You two stay close to his office in case Obi-Wan needs you."

Anakin and Ferus moved off. The crowd was denser now; more beings had arrived. They were louder and giddier. The music was wailing, and some guests were dancing. Anakin could see only bright colors and faces red with a forced gaiety he found distracting. He began to feel an edge of uneasiness. They were risking exposure with every step. His Master was breaking into the secret files of a head of state. And Siri was trying to divert a madman with charm.

Slow down. Breathe. The Force will help you.

"I always hated parties," Ferus said. "I never knew how to have fun at them."

Anakin felt his nerves tighten. He saw Obi-Wan approach the two guards at the corridor's entrance. He waved his hand, and even across the room, Anakin felt the power of the Force.

The guards nodded. Obi-Wan slipped around them and was gone.

"Only a few minutes to go," Anakin said.

Ferus and Anakin waited. When Obi-Wan appeared in the corridor, they were to approach the guards and use the Force to divert them. Then Obi-Wan could simply walk out with the security codes, and they would leave the party. Simple.

Except it wasn't. Two minutes later, the security alarm went off.

CHAPTER ELEVEN

Obi-Wan couldn't believe it. Of course, he was no criminal mastermind, but he felt he was capable, with the help of the Force, of lifting a file of secure codes in a guarded office. He had missed a silent trigger somewhere, one that Joylin's spy hadn't known about.

Any moment the guards would come pounding in. Obi-Wan drove his impatience with himself out of his mind. It was a distraction. He was only halfway through his task. Alarm or no alarm, he had to complete it.

He entered the security code Joylin had given him. He opened the paneled drawer at the side of the ornate desk Teda used. To his surprise, it was a mess. Durasheets, holobooks, disks, wrappers from some sort of sweet. Some of the sweet had melted and pooled in a sticky mess, gluing the durasheets together.

"Nothing worse than a messy dictator," Obi-Wan murmured. He lifted a red slipcase with a disk inside. Joylin had told him that it was the security codes.

The alarm ringing in his ears, he felt the Force surge as the first sentry droids flew through the door. He vaulted over the desk, lightsaber already activated, and cut them down. Four more flew in, firing in a spinning arc that lit up the room with blaster fire. Obi-Wan deflected the fire and charged toward the door. But before he could reach it, a panel rattled down, blocking his exit. Another slid down over the only window. Obviously the plan was to trap the intruder inside with the lethal droids.

Meanwhile, blaster fire continued to ping in transecting lines that were designed to pinpoint his location and blast him to smithereens. Obi-Wan launched himself at the droids, simultaneously taking out Siri's lightsaber and Force-jumping high overhead to cut them down. By the time the droids lay smoking at his feet, he heard the sound of guards outside the door and shuttered window.

Question. Should he cut a hole in the window or door sheeting and charge out, meeting the blasters head on? Or should he wait for them to enter?

Obi-Wan decided to wait. He would have a few seconds of surprise on his side. They would enter expecting to find him dead or badly wounded.

He backed up against a cabinet, out of immediate sightline of the window and doorway. He pressed back against the cabinet. To his surprise, it moved.

He jumped away as the cabinet wall slid back. Becka stood there. Obi-Wan quickly tucked the lightsabers out of sight.

Becka took in the sight of the smoking droids. "Stars and novas, you're good." He beckoned. "This way."

Obi-Wan hesitated.

"If you go out that window, you'll be met with half the security force. The other half is on the other side of that door. They're waiting for the droids to kill you before they open the panels. You've got about twelve seconds. Do you have the codes?"

"Yes." Obi-Wan leaped into the secret passageway. "I assume you're my spy."

"I work with Joylin. We're going to come out in the hallway near the kitchens. Just stay with me."

"I have to find my gang."

"I'd say you have to get out of here, but all right. They might lock down the compound once they find the room is empty."

Becka led him through several turnings. They reached a panel outlined in yellow. He pressed a button and the panel slid open.

Obi-Wan found himself in a small closet, crowded with wraps and cloaks.

Becka opened the door slightly. "Go."

Obi-Wan eased out. Becka followed.

The crowd was nervous. Obi-Wan could smell the panic. No doubt a crowd of criminals did not feel secure when a security alarm was going off. Then it stopped abruptly, and the silence was worse.

"False alarm, folks!" Becka called. "Just enjoy yourselves!" He motioned to the musicians. "Great Leader Teda orders you to keep playing!"

The sight of someone in an official uniform had some effect. The musicians began to play, and the guests began to murmur.

"This way." Becka led Obi-Wan down a hallway and then into the great room from another door. He saw Anakin and Ferus, still monitoring the corridor where Obi-Wan had disappeared. Obi-Wan knew his apprentice was close to charging down the corridor after him.

He hurried over. "It's all right. Becka is going to help us. Where is Valadon?"

"She's outside, ready to cover you in case you come out the window."

Becka, Obi-Wan, Anakin, and Ferus hurried outside. Lights illuminated the wall. Droids buzzed overhead.

They saw Siri on the side of the palace, standing

just outside the ring of guards surrounding the window. The durasteel panel had risen, and some of the guards had leaped inside the room.

Obi-Wan sent out a call to Siri, using the Force. She turned and saw him. He saw the relief on her face. She started toward him.

Becka was watching the placement of the guards carefully. Suddenly, a group of them turned and started toward the gates. Lights began to blink rhythmically on the top of the wall.

"Not good," Becka said. "They're going into lockdown."

Obi-Wan looked around. "Any ideas?"

"I scouted out the back wall," Anakin said. "I think we can make it."

"I don't think you should try it," Becka said. "If they see you, it will just make things harder. Security will be looking for you until they catch you. Leave this to me. All we need is a little panic for cover."

The crowd was on the edge of panic already. They didn't know what was going on. Security guards were now storming through the place, checking ID docs. Flocks of sentry droids buzzed overhead. The sumptuous party had turned into a replica of a prison — a place nobody at the party was particularly interested in revisiting.

"Just wait here for a moment," Becka said.

He went from group to group, speaking quietly. As soon as he left them, the groups talked among themselves, and then to others. Soon, voices began to rise.

"This is outrageous!"

"I will not be detained!"

"I came to this planet for security and peace. . . ."

Becka reappeared at Obi-Wan's side. "Just walk out with the others."

"No one is leaving."

"You lead the way. The guests will follow. I've told them that Teda is keeping them indefinitely for interrogation. They are furious and afraid. Teda will have to let you leave. He depends on their bribes to survive. He won't stop them. You'll see. Go."

Siri looked at Obi-Wan and shrugged. "Worth a try."

Obi-Wan drew his cloak around him. "I for one won't stand for this," he said loudly. "I'm leaving!"

"Yes, let's leave immediately," Siri agreed.

Heads turned. As Obi-Wan and Siri stalked off, followed by Anakin and Ferus, some of the braver guests followed. At first it was a trickle, then a wave.

Everything happened as Becka said it would. The crowd approached the nervous security guards at the gate. They drew their blasters but did not fire them as

Obi-Wan and Siri continued to stride ahead. One officer spoke quickly into a comlink. Obviously, he was contacting Teda.

In just seconds, the security gates opened. Teda could not compromise his treasury by angering those who propped up his regime.

So Obi-Wan and the Jedi left the palace compound in a fashion they hadn't suspected when they'd arrived — leading a large group of angry criminals straight out the front gates.

Joylin was waiting for the Jedi in the prearranged spot, in a narrow alley behind the exclusive shops on the boulevard.

"Heard you had a rough time," Joylin said.

Obi-Wan handed him the codes.

Joylin quickly accessed the small disk and scanned its contents. "It's all worth it." He looked up. "Our operatives are in place. We're going to hit the security center first and knock out the CIP. Then we'll take over the rest."

"Remember," Obi-Wan said, "we want Zan Arbor."

Joylin nodded. "Part of the deal. We won't go back on it. We'll contact you at dawn and you'll tell us how you want to proceed. Your ship will be fueled and you'll have permission to leave, if that's what you want. We have plans to confiscate all other transports, so you'll be the only ones allowed to get off-planet."

Obi-Wan nodded. Good. That way, the Slams would be Zan Arbor's only choice.

"Until then, my suggestion is for you to go back to your villa and lie low. Things are going to get worse before they get better."

"I thought you said this would be a bloodless revolution," Ferus said.

"I said I *intended* it to be," Joylin said. "I still do." He looked overhead. Sentry droids were beginning to patrol the streets, sweeping dark areas with panels of light. "Now I'd better knock out that CIP."

He turned and disappeared down the dark alley. Obi-Wan and Siri exchanged a worried look. They had rarely seen a government takeover that was easy or bloodless.

Yet all they could do was wait.

CHAPTER TWELVE

The Jedi did not take Joylin's advice and return to the villa. They remained on the streets to monitor the progress of the revolt, keeping concealed.

Sentry droids were so thick in the air that a constant humming noise filled the streets. Teda's government was on full alert after the theft in his office.

They knew the instant the CIP had been hit. The sentry droids crashed to the ground, lifeless.

Within minutes, however, the army flooded the streets. The Jedi retreated before them as they headed for Cloudflower Wall, trying to quell the resistance.

They arrived just in time to see the Romin workers burst through the security gates. The mass of beings was like a huge moving mountain. The Jedi were now swept along as the determined group marched toward Teda's palace, pushing the army back in a hard battle.

Obi-Wan had hoped to see joy and liberation on this dark night. Instead, he saw only rage. Sick at heart, the Jedi watched as the looting and violence began. The Romins had been deprived of too much for too long. They had lived with fear as a constant companion. They had watched their children suffer.

The anger fed on itself and grew. They wanted to destroy what had destroyed them.

Transparisteel shattered. Monuments fell. Even trees were hacked down. Fires were lit in the exclusive shops, the businesses that catered to the wealthy, the banks, the assembly halls, even the hospitals. Citizens who had profited from the Teda regime were dragged into the streets and slaughtered.

The Jedi could not be everywhere. It all got out of control too fast.

Siri and Obi-Wan were shaken. They had taken the risk. They had hoped for the best and seen the worst.

Obi-Wan saw the horror through Ferus's eyes. Siri's apprentice grew silent. Obi-Wan saw him shudder as he saw the things he had feared would happen.

"We did this," Ferus said.

"No," Anakin said. "*They* are doing this."

"We have to help," Ferus insisted.

"We'll help where we can," Siri told him. "We can't stop it, Ferus."

They found cowering workers and brought them to shelter. They tended to the wounded and prevented violence where they could.

The night stretched on. The sounds of destruction grew soft as the Romins raged in other parts of the city. They heard the muffled thuds of explosions. The crash of transparisteel. The far-off noise of an alarm. A cry that could have been a bird. But they knew it was not.

By dawn the Jedi had established their villa as an outpost that they guarded from the mob and used to monitor Zan Arbor's villa, which seemed untouched so far. As long as she remained there, Obi-Wan was content to do likewise. Scores of Romin citizens sat in their garden, refugees from homes that had been looted and burned. The Jedi could not begin to sort out who had been involved in Teda's government and who had merely lived and worked in the city. They allowed anyone fleeing to come in and take shelter.

The rising sun brought a kind of calm to the streets. The resistance workers patrolled now, trying to restore order. Obi-Wan and Anakin sat outside, ready for trouble, though they had received no threat for hours now.

"A long night," Anakin said.

"Yes."

"Even after this night, I still think we weren't wrong."

Obi-Wan sighed. He tried to smooth the trampled grass underneath his hand. "Wrong or right — I'm not ready to make that call. We made the decision using the facts we had."

"But we were right," Anakin insisted.

Obi-Wan saw the will Ferus had been talking about, the need to bend the situation to Anakin's own vision of it. The need to be right.

"Anakin, sometimes sureness is not what you should strive for. A little confusion in your mind can be a good thing. Will we be proved right ultimately? I hope so. Did we do the best we could? Yes. That I firmly believe. That's enough for now."

Siri called them from the villa. "The vidscreen is broadcasting. The resistance now has control of the communication system. Joylin is going to speak."

Obi-Wan and Anakin hurried inside. Siri, Ferus, and some of the refugees were crowded around the vid-screen. Others began to pour through the doors, and still others stood outside the windows so that they could hear.

Joylin appeared on the screen. Even on vidscreen, his magnetism was clear. His clothes were stained and rumpled. His face was drawn. Yet strength radiated out from his body, and his eyes were resolute.

"Romin is now in the hands of its people," he said.

A sound rose from the crowd, half gasp, half cry. No one had liked living under Teda. Yet the liberators had come close to destroying the city. How safe were they?

"The Citizens' Resistance is now occupying the palace of the tyrant Teda as well as the government buildings. We have control of communications and trans-portation. Order has been returned to the streets. Some regrettable looting and burning has occurred, but it has been stopped. No one will be granted exit from Romin without the permission of the Citizens' Resis-tance. The army of the Great Leader has deserted or joined us. Let us rejoice, citizens, in our victory. Our tyrant is finished."

A woman standing next to Obi-Wan began to weep. A man turned away, his hand at his mouth.

"Although we begin today as the first day of a gov-ernment of justice and peace, the tyrant who abused our trust, our people, our wealth, our cities, our lands, is still at large. He has fled, like the coward he is."

Obi-Wan and Siri exchanged a glance. So it was not over, then. As long as Teda remained at large, the resistance's hold on the government was shaky at best.

"Teda has fled along with the few who continue to support him. Among them are his chief of staff, General Yubicon, and the galactic criminal Jenna Zan Arbor."

Anakin punched the wall with his fist. It was a rare display of anger. Zan Arbor had slipped through their fingers again.

"Teda is now a wanted criminal. We hereby charge him with crimes against Romin. And so we announce this. We hold the rest of his senior staff and government officials in custody. If Teda does not surrender to us, we will execute them. One by one."

Joylin stared into the camera. His eyes were burning. "Watching, caring, protecting. Roy Teda loves his people. Prove to us you are not a monster. Save those who were loyal to you. And meet the justice of the people you claim to love. We await your surrender. The first execution will take place in one hour. Your first aide, Hansel, will be the first to die."

The screen went to static.

Ferus looked at Obi-Wan. His face was white. He shook his head and turned away.

All night Obi-Wan had consoled himself with the thought that things had to get better with the dawn. Instead, things had gotten worse, more horribly than he could have imagined.

CHAPTER THIRTEEN

Obi-Wan was happy to shed the fine robes of Slam. Siri bundled up her shimmersilk dress, now stained and torn, and threw it away.

"I'm glad to be a Jedi again," she said.

Leaving Anakin and Ferus in charge, they hurried down the deserted streets toward Teda's palace.

"It's not that I'm surprised at what has happened," Obi-Wan told Siri. "It's just that I had hoped for better."

"It is always better to prepare for the worst," Siri said. "I'm glad we contacted Master Windu before the revolt."

"It will still take some time for the Jedi re-enforcements to reach us," Obi-Wan said. "Mace said he would come personally. I don't imagine he'll be in the best of moods. He wasn't happy about this plan from the beginning."

"Neither was Ferus," Siri said. "He was right about the revolt. It got out of control too easily. He thinks if we hadn't helped, maybe they would have postponed the revolt. Maybe Teda would have fallen without being pushed. I tell myself that he doesn't have the experience to realize that sometimes you have to make a hard decision and accept the consequences. And then I think . . . what if he was right?"

"If he was right, then we were wrong," Obi-Wan said. "That's all. Do you think the Jedi are always right?"

Siri sighed. "Sometimes you sound so much like Qui-Gon."

"After all these years, finally a compliment," Obi-Wan said.

He was glad to see that the remark lightened Siri's expression. "Don't let it go to your head," she growled.

"Ferus is wise beyond his years," Obi-Wan went on. "He thinks deeply. But even though an outcome may seem likely, sometimes one has to risk for the right result."

"Yes, Ferus is reluctant to risk too much. Not like Anakin," Siri said. "He's willing to risk everything."

She meant it as a compliment, Obi-Wan knew. Siri admired Anakin's daring, his sureness, how fluidly he used the Force. It was unusual for Siri to second-guess a decision, just like Anakin. In some ways, Obi-Wan was more like Ferus. How odd that he and Anakin had become a team. Their temperaments were so different.

Choose the Master, the Padawan does.

Yoda had said that to him many times, from when he himself was an apprentice. The old Jedi Master believed in most cases that the Force drew the Master and his apprentice together for reasons they couldn't see themselves. Obi-Wan felt strongly that this was true.

Joylin must have been waiting for them, because his security guards let them through without a problem. A tall guard led them to Teda's inner office, where Obi-Wan had stolen the codes. On the way, they saw resistance members wandering about the palace, staring at the fine things. Many had pulled colorful cloaks and tunics over their own threadbare attire. Obviously, they had raided the palace closets. The remnants of the grand party still lay about, food half-eaten on plates, musical instruments abandoned, drinks spilled. There was a strange energy here. The people seemed dazed rather than energized.

Obi-Wan and Siri walked into the inner office. Joylin had cleared out most of the fine furniture and rolled up the rug. Along with an assistant, he was methodically going through Teda's datafiles.

"I have enough here to convict him on state crimes ten times over, and I've only just begun an hour ago," Joylin said. In person, Obi-Wan could see both fatigue and triumph on his face. Joylin didn't look at them, but spoke as he flipped through files. "I suppose you heard about Zan Arbor. She escaped with Teda. Believe me, we tried to trail them. I don't know yet how they got away. Or where they are. Her ship was destroyed when the rioters hit the landing platform. Don't worry — I was able to stop them before they destroyed your ship. I even had it refueled for you."

Joylin looked up at last. "I did what I could. I assume you came for the last half of your payment."

"We don't care about the payment," Obi-Wan said. "We'll give you back what you paid us already. Put it toward restoring the hospital."

For the first time, Joylin seemed to notice the difference in their appearance.

"Who are you?" he asked. His eyes narrowed.

"We are Jedi," Obi-Wan said. "We have the authority of the Senate."

"We've come about the executions you plan," Siri said. "You cannot do this."

Joylin's skin seemed to tighten over his bones. "I am the leader of Romin. I can do anything I want."

"That tone is familiar," Obi-Wan said. "Recognize it, Joylin?"

"I am not Teda," Joylin said. He shook his head at them. "How dare you," he continued softly. "You arrived on my world two days ago. You've seen nothing. You know nothing. You have not seen the prisons, filled to overflowing with those who Teda felt threatened by, filled with those who *displeased* him. You have not seen even one corner of the misery he has caused."

"This does not justify murder," Siri said. "You are judge, jury, and executioner for these people. That goes against galactic law."

"They are all murderers!" Joylin exclaimed. "Don't you understand? If Teda is allowed to go free, we will never be safe. Our movement will collapse. We don't know how many of the army deserted or how many went with him. If I don't do this, we could lose control of the government!"

"Delay," Obi-Wan said. "The Jedi can help you. More are arriving."

"I did not call for the Jedi."

"I did," Obi-Wan said. "The Senate has approved."

Joylin stood. "This is my world," he said, his voice steely. "I have worked and sacrificed for twenty years to stand here. I will not risk the collapse of a government by the people."

"Excuse me," Obi-Wan replied. "From where we are standing, it appears that you *are* the government."

Joylin planted his fists on the desk and leaned forward. His face was composed, but his eyes shone bright and hostile.

"Your interference is unwelcome. I have nothing more to say. Go, or I'll have you thrown out."

Obi-Wan was perfectly aware that no one in the palace had the power to throw them out. Yet a battle now would do no good. He and Siri turned and walked out.

On the way back to the villa, they talked over what to do next. It was clear that they had antagonized Joylin. They didn't know how much longer he would allow them to remain on Romin. That didn't mean they had to leave. It would just make things more difficult.

"I think our best bet is to find Teda," Obi-Wan said. "If Zan Arbor is with him, it will solve two of our problems."

"Agreed," Siri said. "But where can we look where Joylin's people haven't already?"

They walked past the gates of the villa. Ferus hurried toward them.

"We just received a message," he said. "It's from Teda and Zan Arbor. They request a meeting with the Slams. And since the revolt took place before the real Slams met Teda, that's us."

CHAPTER FOURTEEN

Teda and Zan Arbor were at a safe house well out-side the city. The Jedi borrowed a Gian airspeeder from one of the refugees they'd taken in. The house was in a forest so densely wooded that they had to abandon the speeder and hike in to the prearranged coordi-nates. They were met by General Yubicon, Teda's chief of staff.

"It's just a quarter kilometer this way," he said.

Anakin could tell that the general led them in a way designed to confuse them. He did not realize he was dealing with Jedi. Anakin knew he could find his way back easily.

They came to a small clearing. The house in front of them was made of prefabricated plasteel materials so it could be dismantled and moved quickly. That must have been Teda's secret. His safe house never stayed in the same place.

Guards encircled the house. Anakin knew more were positioned in the woods. He couldn't see them, but he knew they were there. Obviously, Teda had retained at least part of his army.

A guard at the door ushered them in. They were expected.

The house was tiny compared to the palace, but it was not rustic. It was furnished sparely but lavishly, with plush seating and thick rugs. The rooms flowed into each other, forming a square around a central courtyard that was open to the sky. They were led to the courtyard, where they found Teda and Jenna Zan Arbor waiting for them.

Teda seemed a bit shaken, but Zan Arbor was composed. Not a hair of her perfect coiffure was out of place. Wearing his mask once more, Anakin kept to the rear with Ferus as Obi-Wan and Siri moved forward. As one of the lesser members of the Slam gang, he hoped to escape Zan Arbor's notice completely. He still remembered the intense focus she had given him as she questioned him about the Force. He wasn't afraid of her, but he wouldn't mind staying out of her way.

As Anakin expected, Teda and Zan Arbor were totally focused on Siri and Obi-Wan, the leaders of the gang. The Jedi had changed back into their Slam wardrobes. Siri was wearing another revealing robe, this time in a pale pink. She had complained about having to don her attire again, but you'd never know it now by the way she drifted forward and let her hand rest in Teda's in greeting. You'd never suspect that she held the leader in contempt as she smiled, turned so that her skirt flared out, and settled herself in a chair, coyly crossing her legs. Obi-Wan, too, managed to continue his part of the farce, smiling graciously as he sat to the sound of his jingling robes.

"Thank you for coming," Teda said. "Of course you realize that this so-called revolt of the people is a temporary situation only. It will all go away, I assure you."

"But that is not why you are here," Zan Arbor said, obviously bored by the subject of the revolt. "You came to me yesterday and offered me a chance to join you in an enterprise. Unfortunately, I had to refuse you. Now I ask for the chance to tempt you instead."

Obi-Wan tilted his head. "I'll try to forgive you for refusing me. Please continue."

Siri gave Teda a glance through her eyelashes. "I love to be tempted."

Zan Arbor looked annoyed at Siri's flirtatiousness. "Teda and I have been working together on a certain enterprise —"

"Excuse me," Teda said. "But I haven't lost my title, you know."

Out of Teda's sight line, Zan Arbor rolled her eyes. "*Great Leader* Teda and I are partners together in an enterprise. Because of the sudden, surprising nature of the revolt, even though there was enough warning if you were clever enough to catch it, and the complete inability of Romin's supposedly great army to retaliate —"

Interesting, Anakin thought. *Zan Arbor isn't afraid of Teda in the least. She's taunting him, right to his face. And he's taking it.*

"— we find ourselves in a situation in which we are in need of your help. Thus we are able to offer you a chance to join with us. In short, we need false text docs, very complete, which I understand is your specialty."

"That would not be a problem," Obi-Wan said. "We just need access to our ship and our files. Our ship has survived the revolt, I'm happy to say."

"Mine did not," Zan Arbor said, flicking an angry gaze at Teda. "It was a Luxe Flightwing. Completely destroyed."

"Ah. So you are stranded on Romin." Obi-Wan clucked his tongue. "How unfortunate."

"Naturally, we will pay you your normal fee," Teda said.

"Or a little more," Obi-Wan said with a grin. "Considering the circumstances."

Zan Arbor nodded, an acceptance of Obi-Wan's point that they had no one else to turn to. "We also need your heist skills for a particular job. Or rather, this is not just a job. It's an opportunity to change your lives. The scope of it means that if we are successful, you can retire and live very well for the rest of your lives."

"We already live well," Siri pointed out.

"You will live better," Zan Arbor snapped.

"And you will not be a fugitive," Teda said in a voice like honey. "You will have plenty of systems to choose from to live in." He winked at Siri. "Just tell me where you choose, so I can visit."

"In other words, you are in the right place at the right time, for once," Zan Arbor said. "You have a chance to change your destiny as small-time crooks."

"Jenna, Jenna," Teda chided. "You are talking about the Slams. They are brilliant masterminds."

Zan Arbor waved a hand. "I mean no disrespect. I speak the truth. I am offering them something they would never be able to contemplate by themselves. Slam, even though you lie for a living, you should respect that I won't lie to you. Now, where is your ship?"

"It's at the main landing platform. Fueled and ready."

"Good. So, are you in?"

"Whoa, let's pull back on the throttle a bit. I haven't heard enough yet," Obi-Wan said. Anakin knew what his Master was thinking. He had to get more information, information that Zan Arbor and Teda wouldn't want to part with. This must be the scheme that Zan Arbor was working on with Granta Omega.

"We're intrigued," Siri chimed in. "We need a few more details. What is the nature of the job?"

"You don't need to know that yet," Zan Arbor said.

"Are you well financed?" Obi-Wan asked.

"That is not a problem," Zan Arbor assured him.

"Do you have other partners?" Obi-Wan asked.

"One other," Zan Arbor said reluctantly.

Siri fixed her blue gaze on Teda. "I hope that this partner's stature is as great as yours. Though I can't imagine it."

"It is," Teda boasted, before Zan Arbor could stop him. "He is the most powerful business power in the galaxy. He —"

"That is enough," Zan Arbor interrupted. She turned to Obi-Wan. "Now, our first step is to get off-planet. We must get to your vehicle."

"Have you heard Joylin's ultimatum?" Obi-Wan

asked Teda. "He is threatening to execute your loyal officers. Hansel is the first."

"I heard. Oh, poor Hansel. I feel so very badly for him," Teda said with a sigh. He rubbed his hands together. "Now, are you sure you have enough fuel? We are traveling to the Core, to Coruscant."

"Coruscant?" Obi-Wan asked.

"Teda, be quiet," Zan Arbor snapped, her voice hard. "Who is your text doc expert?" she asked Obi-Wan.

"Waldo," Obi-Wan said, indicating Anakin.

Zan Arbor turned. The sun came out from behind a cloud, and Anakin felt suddenly exposed in the bright light, even with his headgear disguise.

A long moment ticked by. Anakin felt uncomfortably warm. The Force suddenly surged. A warning.

"I know you," she said.

"I don't believe so."

"We have crossed paths."

"Perhaps," Obi-Wan said. "We've traveled widely."

"Joylin has closed down the spaceport, but we have received permission to leave," Siri interrupted. "However, we must do it within the hour. Can you be ready?"

"I am ready now," Zan Arbor said. Her attention slid away from Anakin. There were more pressing matters to deal with.

"Then let us go," Obi-Wan said.

There was a commotion outside. Teda leaped to his feet, a blaster in his hand. The Jedi turned.

The real Slam and the rest of his gang burst into the courtyard. Slam pointed a finger at Obi-Wan.

"Impostors!" he cried.

CHAPTER FIFTEEN

Teda looked alarmed, but Zan Arbor suddenly smiled, as if she had just figured something out. She turned back to Anakin.

"Jedi," she said. "Now I remember."

Now Teda looked panicky. "Jedi?"

She rose and drew closer to Anakin, ignoring the Slams and the other Jedi. "Good disguise. But it isn't your face that beings remember. It's your manner. Your power. The way you move. I remembered you after our visit together on Vanqor. I asked about you. Teda, don't you admire me for recognizing that this scruffy prisoner, one among so many, was different? You're Anakin Skywalker."

She gazed at him with a hungry expression. Anakin felt unnerved.

"I have studied the Force for so long," she murmured. "Never did I expect such a prize."

"I'm not your prize," he spat out.

"Well, you're my prisoner, and that's the same thing. Do you know how many guards are surrounding you right now?"

Obi-Wan shot Anakin a look. The Jedi could fight. They could escape. But Obi-Wan was telling him to wait. They had more to discover. The stakes were too high.

"We can take them to the prison and have them executed on the spot," Teda said.

"Don't be so hasty," Zan Arbor said.

"Look, you don't have to kill them," Slam said, looking uneasy now. "Just tell them to stop impersonating us."

Valadon, as tall as Siri and as blond, shot her an icy look. "And give us our clothes back."

Zan Arbor had not taken her eyes off Anakin. "Do you know what we have here, Teda?"

"Yes," he moaned. "A big headache."

"Leverage. Remember our discussion before? If we bring a great prize to our partner, he will look at us differently. We can negotiate a different split."

"What are you talking about, Jenna?" Teda asked impatiently. "Prizes? Leverage? Please remember I am a ruling ruler who was just kicked out of his palace. I'm not in the best of moods!"

"The Chosen One," Zan Arbor said softly to Anakin, so that no one else could hear. "I was told about you. My interest in the Force is deep. Enough to know how your destiny is your burden. Do you remember the Zone of Self-Containment? I can bring that back to you."

He remembered feeling content, a contentment without a tether to sadness or guilt. There was just the sun and serenity, a serenity he had never achieved as a Jedi. The Jedi had promised him that, and it had not happened. Perhaps it never would.

"Ah," she said softly, "speaking of temptation . . ."

He pulled off the mask. There was no need for it now. "I'm not tempted by you," he responded.

"I saw how you enjoyed it," she said. "I can make all your burdens disappear."

"My only burden at the moment is having to talk to you," Anakin shot back.

She smiled. Anakin could see that once, before evil had twisted her, she had been seductive. Her smile was lush, appreciative, inviting.

"You remind me of someone I knew a long time ago," she said.

Obi-Wan overheard that. "Qui-Gon Jinn," he said.

Zan Arbor whirled around. She walked closer to Obi-Wan. "Do I know you?"

"Obi-Wan Kenobi."

She laughed in delight. "Obi-Wan! But you were just a boy! You've grown up well," she said, appraising him. "I heard Qui-Gon died on Naboo. And Yaddle has recently 'joined the Force,' hasn't she — a Jedi Council member? It makes you think, doesn't it?" She shook her head. "What is happening to the Jedi? Their strength diminishing, their best leaders struck down. And yet they don't see that they are declining. Such a pity to watch. So intriguing to study."

Anakin saw Siri's eyes flash. She did not speak. He knew from experience that she did not spar with villains. She just waited her turn. She was absolutely certain at all times that she would prevail in the end. He liked that certainty. He held an image in his mind of Zan Arbor back on a prison world while he, Obi-Wan, Siri, and Ferus watched her being led away. He needed to hold on to that vision.

"Jenna, we need to plan a plan," Teda said irritably.

"Oh, Roy, relax," Zan Arbor said. She waved at the tea table, indicating the Slams. "Slam, Valadon, have some refreshment. We need to talk. You are going to transport us off the planet — don't worry, we know where your transport is — and we have a proposition for you that the Jedi have already accepted on your behalf."

Easygoing as always, Slam pulled a chair up to the table and poured himself some tea. "This is sounding more promising. How happy I am that your messengers found me."

"Meanwhile," Zan Arbor said, "Teda, call the rest of your guards — and I mean all of them. I want General Yubicon in charge."

"But he's my personal bodyguard now!"

"Oh, don't be such a baby. I am tired of your whining." She turned to the Jedi. "They have superior weaponry, I assure you. And if you don't want anyone else harmed, you'll do best to comply." She gave a pointed look at the Slams. It was clear she would sacrifice them if the Jedi did not cooperate.

The guards moved closer. Teda spoke into a comlink and they heard the humming of swoops as more guards took to the air. They hovered above the courtyard. Anakin saw blaster rifles pointed at them — and Slam, Valadon, and the other members of the gang.

"Your lightsabers," Zan Arbor said. "Give them to General Yubicon."

Obi-Wan slipped his and Siri's lightsabers out of his belt and handed them over. Ferus and Anakin followed. Anakin knew his Master would never hand over his lightsaber unless he was fully intending to get it back shortly.

"Put the lightsabers in the prison vault," Zan Arbor ordered the general. "I'll want to study them. Put the prisoners in the holding cell for now and have them guarded severely. We'll pick them up as soon as we finish here." She leveled her icy gaze on General Yubicon. "Don't let them out of your sight, don't listen to them, and don't make any mistakes. Go."

General Yubicon's eyes flickered as he stuffed the lightsabers into a satchel that he slung on his back. Anakin could see that he did not like taking orders from Zan Arbor. Teda didn't say a word. Anakin realized who was truly in charge. Zan Arbor had Teda under her thumb.

Slam cocked his head at them. "Sorry. I didn't mean for it to go quite this far. But all's fair."

"That's very true," Obi-Wan said. "If you join up with these two, you'll get what you deserve."

The Jedi were roughly herded out of the house and pushed along a rutted road that ran through woods with branches so thick with dark green leaves that they blotted out the sun completely.

They were marched farther down the path — playing along for now, waiting for the right moment to turn the tables. The area felt desolate and dank. Over the thump of footsteps and the buzzing of the swoops overhead, Anakin saw General Yubicon speaking to his assistant as they walked. He called on the Force to help him tune out the noises around him and focus on what the officer was saying.

". . . thought we had a strong leader, but he is just as much a sham as they say he is. Am I supposed to pledge my loyalty now to Great Leader Zan Arbor?"

"What can you do?" the other officer asked in disgust. "One day we're living in a palace in Romin, the next in the middle of a swamp. It's enough to make me join the resistance."

"And what would the resistance do to you if they found you?" the first officer said. "Look what they're doing to poor Hansel. Listen, we're safer with Teda. Or at least I thought so. Now I suspect that Zan Arbor is planning to take off with him and without us. Teda said he would take his first officers, but will she let him? They're planning something big. Teda said they will have the Senate to do their bidding."

The Senate? Anakin gave a quick glance at Obi-Wan. He could tell his Master was listening, as well.

"Here we are," the other officer said. "Mind yourself. The prisoners know something is up, somehow. They're restless. Not to mention starving."

"Just be glad you're not in their place," General Yubicon said.

The prison rose ahead, long and low, built of dark green duracrete so that it would not be visible from above or from the road. The resistance had not gotten here yet. The Jedi passed through energy gates and into the compound. A door rose into the ceiling to admit them.

The inside of the prison stank of dirt and rot. There were no windows. A security console ran along a blank wall. Droids that had not been affected by the revolt in the city sat monitoring the equipment. Their sensors flashed green as General Yubicon entered.

Energy cages hung suspended from the ceiling. The walls and floors were stained with dark matter. Desperation and pain seemed to be as much a part of this structure as durasteel and duracrete.

Obi-Wan looked at Anakin.

Not yet, but soon.

The guards flooded in behind them. Now they would not have to deal with the swoops overhead.

The guards opened a second door, which also rose vertically. Behind an energy fence was an enormous cell. It was stuffed full of beings and aliens from many worlds. Most of them wore rags and were barefoot. They eyed the guards with hatred. Some of them looked cheered at the prospect of breaking in new prisoners.

"When, Master?" Anakin asked urgently.

"It seems to me," Ferus said politely, "that now would be an extremely good time."

"Okay," Obi-Wan said. "Now."

The four Jedi moved as one. There were twenty-two army officers in the prison and five prison droids within their sight. No doubt more droids were in the inner rooms of the prison. But now was as good a time as any to attack.

Obi-Wan, Ferus, and Anakin went for the officers, using the Force to push the first line with such power that they bowled over their fellow officers. Blaster shots went wild and pinged on the prison walls. Siri whirled and kicked General Yubicon in the chest, knocking him backward. His head hit the duracrete floor, knocking him out with the stunned expression still on his face. She leaned over, deftly plucked the lightsabers from the satchel, and tossed them to the Jedi.

Anakin leaped above the guards. He grabbed the bottom of an energy cage and flipped himself in a midair somersault, then landed behind them. From there it was easy to simply disarm two officers before they had a chance to turn around. Without their weapons, the guards turned, looked at General Yubicon on the floor, and simply ran out.

Lightsabers blazing, the Jedi advanced through the rest of the officers and droids, deflecting fire. Behind them, the prisoners roared approval.

Then Anakin heard a voice above the rest, coming from the holding cell. The prisoners were shouting, and it took him a moment to make out the words. "The stun nets!"

More guards flooded the main room, stun net launchers in hand. They didn't care that they would snare other guards. They let loose the nets with their electrical charges. The nets hung in the air for a split second. In a blink of an eye they would blanket the room.

In that split second Anakin made his calculations. He knew if they were hit with the nets, the paralyzing charges could hamper them. The nets would ensnare them, and every time they moved, sensors would deliver another paralyzing charge. Better to avoid them completely then slash away with their lightsabers. The nets wouldn't stop them, but they would slow them down.

He stepped forward before the others could move. He held up a hand. He felt the Force in the room. Could he do it? He reached out with his mind, gathering in the Force. He thought of his lessons with Soara Antana. Everything in the prison became fluid to him. It was easy to move, easy to manipulate.

Using the Force, he flipped each of the nets back-ward and onto the guards.

The guards fell, shouting and kicking. Within mo-ments, they were still, unwilling to cause another charge to jolt them.

The prisoners sent up a roar.

Suddenly, the prison wall began to glow. A red line appeared on the wall, moving upward quickly.

"The army must be outside," Obi-Wan said. "They're using laser artillery. Watch out . . . the wall is going to come down!"

They leaped backward as the entire entry wall sud-denly fell with a crash, exposing the prison to the woods beyond.

Then they got the bad news. Outside was an entire battalion of soldiers.

"Surrender!" an amplified voice cried.

"Let us out!" one of the prisoners cried. "Let us fight!"

Obi-Wan leaped over and deactivated the energy fence. The prisoners rushed out, grabbing blaster rifles and stun batons from the fallen guards.

"We can do it. Just give us a chance." A short Romin in a tattered tunic stood next to Obi-Wan, a blaster in his fist.

"We didn't free you to see you slaughtered," Obi-Wan said. "That's an army out there. With grenade mortars and missile tubes."

"Surrender or die!" the voice repeated.

Anakin looked at the prisoners. Their faces were grim. They were ready to face whatever came.

"Do what you want," the prisoner said. "We've been inside too long. We won't surrender."

"We can win, Master," Anakin urged.

"There has to be a weapons room," Obi-Wan said rapidly to Anakin. "Go with Ferus. Bring back what you find."

Anakin motioned to Ferus, and they leaped over the guards in the stun nets and ran down the hall. It wasn't hard to find the weapons room. They found blaster rifles and more stun net launchers. The prisoners crowded in with them, quickly grabbing blaster rifles and stun batons. Anakin picked up a flamethrower. Then he and Ferus hurried back to Obi-Wan and Siri with the stun nets.

"They're re-forming their battle line," Obi-Wan said. "They want to risk as few soldiers as possible. These stun nets can come in handy. But they don't have much range."

"You wouldn't have to worry about range from a

swoop," Ferus said. "There are some outside the front door."

"You'll get blasted into the sky if you stick a toe out there," Obi-Wan said.

"Cover me," Ferus said.

Anakin would have just run. But Ferus waited to get Siri's nod. He dashed toward the front of the building.

"Anakin, use that flamethrower launcher," Obi-Wan said. "Don't hit the front line. Just keep it moving along so they back up. Try to drive them between those trees so that Ferus can drop the nets. Siri, come on."

Anakin powered up the flamethrower while Siri and Obi-Wan ran out. The army began to fire. Using wrist rockets and small missiles, the army tried to advance, as Anakin concentrated the flamethrower on the center of the line.

Siri and Obi-Wan Force-jumped past the flames, aiming their lightsabers at the weapons the troops had left behind as they hurried to escape.

Ferus flew overhead, piloting the swoop with one hand on the bars, using his knees to steer. With astonishing speed, he activated the net launchers, one after the other, and tossed them over the front lines.

The soldiers fell, and the others behind were confused. They looked to their captain, but he had been diverted and was ordering the others to put out the fire that had started in the brush. Smoke began to roll over the soldiers, making them cough.

Obi-Wan looked back at the prisoners. He held up a hand. "Now!" he shouted.

With a cry, the prisoners surged forward. The Jedi had succeeded in confusing and disorienting the army. But it had not vanquished them. Mortar fire pounded and blaster fire shuddered. The Jedi moved, leading the charge, deflecting fire when they could and Force-pushing the troops away.

Anakin felt his blood pumping with the challenge of facing an army. He felt certain of victory, yet he also saw that it would be difficult. Obi-Wan had been right. What kind of a victory would they have if the prisoners were slaughtered? They were falling around him, no matter how quickly he moved, no matter how many missile launchers he took out. There were too few Jedi and too many weapons.

Just then, a sleek cruiser glowed red in the sky. It dropped down like a stone to a perfect landing, like a feather on a blade of grass. Anakin felt a surge of relief. There were only two or three Jedi he knew who could land a plane like that. He was one of them. Another was Garen Muln, Obi-Wan's old friend.

The ramp slid down. Mace Windu, Bant Aerin, and Garen Muln charged down the ramp. Their lightsabers were a blur as they moved through the troops.

The Force was strong now, compounded by them all fighting at the peak of concentration. They joined together, strategically targeting the army so that they separated divisions from each other and knocked out the leaders who tried to organize.

Within a short time, the tide of the battle turned. When the captain of the troops found himself facing the Jedi personally, he laid down his weapon and surrendered.

When the rest of the army threw down their weapons, Anakin could almost hear the sighs of relief. Everyone was tired of fighting. Everyone just wanted to go home.

CHAPTER SIXTEEN

"Rescuing you is becoming a habit," Garen said to Obi-Wan.

Bant smiled her shy smile. "This time I came along for the ride."

Obi-Wan put his hands on her shoulders. He did not say a word. They smiled at each other. He hadn't seen Bant in three years. They had worked out a system of communication, however. Whenever one of them was at the Temple, they would leave the other a message or a small gift. A river stone, a sweet, a dried flower, an odd turn of phrase they had learned in a new language, written on a folded durasheet and tied with a bit of fabric. So Obi-Wan had continued to feel her gentle presence in his life. But seeing her was better.

"If you two wouldn't mind curtailing the reunion, I'd

like a status report." Mace's voice was dry. It was clear that he wasn't very happy about having to disrupt his schedule to fly to Romin.

"First of all, the real Slam gang is on Romin," Obi-Wan said.

"I know," Mace replied. "Apparently they bribed the director of the prison."

"Teda and Zan Arbor are scheming to get off-planet," Siri said. "They're going to try to use the Slams' ship. Joylin is still in power. The first execution is scheduled to take place in . . . about fifteen minutes."

"Then I think our first task is to demonstrate to Great Leader Teda the necessity of his surrender," Mace said.

They caught Zan Arbor and Teda as Teda was attempting to start an airspeeder piled high with cases and boxes. Garen landed the transport directly in front of them.

"Do it!" Zan Arbor was shouting.

"I'm usually *driven*," Teda said. "I don't usually *drive*."

"For galaxy's sake, let me drive!" Zan Arbor yelled.

Mace Windu swept up and buried his lightsaber in the airspeeder's engine, effectively cutting off power in one stroke. "Don't worry. You can ride with us."

Zan Arbor's lips were white. Fury was evident in the strained muscles of her neck. Her veins protruded like ropes. "Jedi," she spat out.

"What did you do to my army?" Teda asked. "No one is answering my communications. You can't interfere with a sovereign power!"

"What's left of your army has been destroyed and your commander has surrendered," Mace said. "And I'm afraid I *do* have the authority to interfere. I am here on behalf of the Senate to negotiate the terms of your surrender."

"I will never surrender!" Teda cried.

Zan Arbor began to climb out of the airspeeder. "I'm not part of this, so I think I'll —"

Mace Windu held his blazing lightsaber centimeters from her face. "I think," he said softly, "you'll do as you're told."

Zan Arbor backed up and sat on the edge of the airspeeder.

"Now," Mace Windu said, "where are the Slams?"

"How should we know?" Zan Arbor said sulkily.

"My guess is that they've gone to get their ship," Siri said. "No doubt they have plans to meet and transport Zan Arbor and Teda off-planet."

"Here's what's going to happen," Mace Windu said.

"We're going to escort you to the headquarters of the new government of Romin."

"You mean bring me to my own palace?" Teda asked with a sneer. "So I can negotiate with thieves and murderers? Is that what the Senate sanctions these days?"

"The Senate is supporting this revolt on the basis of your many crimes against your own citizens," Mace thundered. "You are lucky the Jedi are here to ensure you won't be torn limb from limb. Now let's go."

Joylin was sitting with his closest allies eating a large meal in the dining area when the Jedi arrived with Teda and Zan Arbor in tow. He pushed away his food and stood.

"So, you came," he said, looking at Teda with hatred. "Not by choice, I see. Typical of your cowardice."

Teda looked at the meal. "That's my food!"

"It is the food of the citizens of Romin."

Zan Arbor rolled her eyes. "Ah, democracy," she sneered.

"Here is what the Senate requires," Mace said. "No executions may take place. Trials must be held, evidence gathered. You cannot begin a new government using the tactics of the one you overthrew. Surely you can see that."

Joylin said nothing. He stared with hatred at Teda.

"Give the order to stop the execution," Mace said.

Joylin did not move.

"The Jedi have destroyed Teda's army," Mace said. "Would you like us to do the same to yours?"

Ferus spoke. "Senate support will be crucial in building your new world," he said to Joylin. "You have done so much. Your vision deserves the best chance to flourish."

Joylin turned. He blinked at Ferus, as though he had been disturbed out of a deep sleep. "Yes," he said. He picked up his comlink. "Stop the execution. Teda has surrendered."

"I hope you won't be putting me with the others," Teda said. "I wouldn't think they'd be very . . . pleased to see me."

"I think it's the perfect place for you," Joylin said. "Guards!"

The guards led Teda and Zan Arbor away. Joylin leaned over to speak to an aide on the other side of the room.

"I feel sorrow that lives were lost, but the outcome is good," Mace said to the Jedi. "This change on Romin will make a better world."

He turned to Ferus. "You spoke well just now. You allowed Joylin to make his decision and save face in front of his supporters."

"There is a bit of pride mixed in with his politics," Ferus said.

"Ferus showed a greater grasp of this situation than we did," Siri said lightly. "He predicted a chaotic takeover. He said that Joylin would surprise us, and he was right."

"Good, Ferus. We need to anticipate problems," Mace said.

Obi-Wan noted that Anakin looked unhappy. Mace had singled Ferus out for praise. He moved closer to his Padawan.

"I am proud of you," he said. "You fought well, with compassion and precision."

But Anakin was not listening.

Something was wrong.

CHAPTER SEVENTEEN

Anakin hung back, watching Joylin carefully. He knew the Force was helping him, he knew that this sudden power was a new side of the Force that he hadn't yet tapped, and he was filled with a sudden sense of exultation. He had even more power than he knew. Suddenly, he saw into the heart of Joylin. He did not see just what Joylin wanted them to see, or didn't care if they saw, but the most secret part of him. Joylin suddenly looked so small. He was such easy prey.

I didn't know this, Anakin thought. *The Force isn't just about manipulating objects. I can manipulate beings, too. I can use their fears and secrets.*

"You did it," he said to Joylin. "You let him go."

The Jedi turned to look at him, surprised.

"Those guards aren't taking Teda to prison. You never wanted him to surrender," Anakin said. "You knew he was too much of a coward to do so. You just gave him the ultimatum so you would have an excuse to execute all his loyal followers. You were afraid if they survived they would build a power base and ultimately destroy you. You knew that Teda was nothing without them, that he wasn't capable of running a government. He's just a figurehead. You don't fear him, so you don't need him dead. You just need him gone. So if someone like Zan Arbor pays you enough, you'll allow him to escape. She made the deal with you at the beginning of the revolt, didn't she?"

The Jedi turned back to Joylin. His angry silence told them everything.

"Where are they?" Mace asked.

"I'd guess Teda and Zan Arbor are heading for the Slams' ship," Anakin said. "And I would also guess that the Slams have permission to leave Romin, no matter what Joylin has told us. He has kept the permission order for the Slams to leave in place despite the lockdown."

"Withdraw that permission," Mace ordered.

"It is too late," Joylin replied.

With a withering look of contempt at Joylin, Mace led the Jedi out of the room.

They rushed to the landing platform, zooming up in one of the turbolifts. When they reached the top, the Jedi quickly hid behind a gravsled stacked with equipment. They could see the Slams readying the ship for departure. Through a windscreen, Anakin saw a blond head.

"They are still here," Mace said. "Excellent work, Anakin. Let's go."

"Wait." Obi-Wan's tone was sharp, and Mace turned, surprised. He was rarely told to wait.

"We should let them go," Obi-Wan said. "This is our chance. They are on their way to Granta Omega. It's the only way we can find him. If we can get a tracking device aboard, we'll have him."

"Obi-Wan, we have Zan Arbor here, now," Mace said. "She is capable of doing great harm to many. Are you willing to risk letting her go for the sake of Granta Omega?"

"I feel strongly that we must," Obi-Wan said. "Omega is the bigger threat."

Ferus bit his lip, looking from Obi-Wan to Mace. Anakin waited, his hand on his lightsaber.

Siri's eyes blazed in agreement. "Obi-Wan is right. Ferus and I are ready to join them on this mission," she told Mace.

"I do not know that you're correct," Mace said. "A

position I find myself in all too often these days. If you feel strongly, Obi-Wan, I support your decision. But everything depends on getting that tracking device on the ship without being seen."

Obi-Wan turned to Anakin with such confidence, such assurance, that Anakin felt he would never forget this moment. Trust lay between them, unbreakable.

"Anakin?"

"I will do it, Master."

He took a tracking device out of his utility belt and stood. Keeping behind the supplies, the gravsleds, and fueling trucks, he slid in as close as he dared. He would have to choose his moment. A moment when no one aboard would be looking.

The Force. He could use it. He wasn't sure how. But he reached out for it and gathered it, formed it to his pleasure, to what he needed.

The engines fired. He was close enough to feel their heat. *Now.*

The ship rose, just a meter above the ground, hovering for the few crucial seconds needed to input coordinates and information. With the help of the Force, those seconds spun out into more time, enough time for him.

Anakin used the Force to jump straight toward the exhaust, where no viewscreens could see him. The temperature was blazing hot, too hot for a living being to stand, yet he stood it and it did not burn him. He was close to the edge of the landing platform here. He timed the move as the ship rose. With a grunt and a call to the Force for help, he tossed the tracking device as the ship lifted. He saw it catch on the underside. When the ship rotated, Anakin was already back behind the fuel pump, jumping down perfectly with not a millimeter to spare.

The Slams' ship shot out of sight.

Anakin rose. His legs felt slightly shaky at the dangerous maneuver. His skin felt hot, but he knew he wasn't burned. Mace and the others walked toward him.

Mace looked at him, his dark eyes raking him. "Impressive."

"Are you hurt?" Obi-Wan asked him. "I didn't mean for you to jump into the ship's exhaust funnels."

"I'm not hurt."

Mace looked up at the vapor trail the ship had left. "I hope we made the right decision," he said. "Are you ready to track them?"

"Yes," Obi-Wan said. "Granta has always been one step ahead of us. He has always planned our meetings. Now I will decide how we next meet."

"May the Force be with you." Mace started away.

"Uh, Master Windu?" Obi-Wan said. Mace turned and gave him an impatient look.

"Just one more thing," Obi-Wan continued. "We need your ship."

Siri sat at the controls. They had been traveling for days now, following the pulse of the tracking device. The Slams' ship was heading into the vast empty space of the Outer Rim.

Ferus had stretched out on his sleep couch. He would take the next piloting shift. Obi-Wan sat at the table in the eating area. He had spread out a number of holofiles, information about Granta Omega gathered by Archivist Jocasta Nu at the Temple. Obi-Wan knew the information by heart, but he still didn't believe it was possible to study it too deeply.

Anakin sat, staring out the viewscreen at the stars. He was in a place of deep quiet, not meditation, exactly, but open to the galaxy, to the energy that boiled from stars and worlds, satellites, matter and nonmatter, gravity, inertia, living beings.

Suddenly, he sat erect. Every muscle tensed.

Obi-Wan looked up. "What is it?"

Anakin turned to him.

"Omega. He knows we are coming.